THE YEAR'S 25 FINEST
CRIME & MYSTERY STORIES
Sixth Annual Edition

THE YEAR'S 25 FINEST CRIME & MYSTERY STORIES

Sixth Annual Edition

Edited by

Joan Hess
Ed Gorman
Martin H. Greenberg

Introduction by Jon L. Breen
With an Overview by Edward D. Hoch

Carroll & Graf Publishers, Inc.
New York

First Carroll & Graf edition 1997

Carroll & Graf Publishers, Inc.
19 West 21st St., Suite 601
New York, NY 10010

ISBN: 0-7867-0495-0
ISSN: 1089-6430

Manufactured in the United States of America

PERMISSIONS

CONTENTS

THE YEAR'S 25 FINEST
CRIME & MYSTERY STORIES
Sixth Annual Edition

Introduction
THE MYSTERY IN 1996

If I decide to call 1996 mystery fiction's Year of the Internet, some of you will say, "Oh, sure, now that the Last of the Luddites has finally gotten on line, he's going to declare a great discovery something the rest of us have known about for years," while others will ask mournfully, "Can't I turn anywhere without hearing about the [overhyped, addictive, dangerous, soul-devouring] Internet?"

But consider the facts. Many of the field's major institutions (Mystery Writers of America, Bouchercon, Malice Domestic, Sisters in Crime, Crime Writers Association) now have their own websites (or is it homepages?— a subtle difference I don't choose to worry about), providing not only a vehicle for advertising, but instant access to recent and past award winners and other current information. Many publishers and mystery writers also use the Internet as an advertising and informational medium. But here's what secured my conversion to online culture: I found an unsigned (and very knowledgable, i.e., complimentary) critical analysis of my own writing I didn't even know existed.

Those of a nostalgic bent should be aware that mystery fiction's past is sometimes honored in cyberspace more reverently than in print. There are, for example, homepages (or do I mean websites?) devoted to Harry Stephen Keeler and to August Derleth's Sherlock Holmes pastiche, Solar Pons, along with many other past writers and characters. I'll resist the urge to litter this page with a lot of www's and .com's—Yahoo or any of the other search engines (if that's the right term) will get you there as quickly.

If you don't like Year of the Internet, how about Yet Another Year of Sherlock Holmes? That the Edgar winner in the biographical/critical category was a Holmesian study, Michael Atkinson's *The Secret Marriage of Sherlock Holmes* (University of Michigan Press), is just one indication of what a bumper year it was for the Baker Street sleuth one hundred and ten years after his birth in print.

Whenever I start to wonder why I persist in reading and collecting Sherlock Holmes pastiches—after all, isn't the Doyle canon of four novels and fifty-six stories enough?—a bunch of books come along to reaffirm my faith. To begin with, there were two outstanding original anthologies of short stories: *Holmes for the Holidays* (Berkley), edited by Martin H. Greenberg, Jon L. Lellenberg, and Carol-Lynn Waugh, in which writers as various as Anne Perry, Loren D. Estleman, Carole Nelson Douglas, and Reginald Hill essay new Sherlockian Christmas stories; and *Resurrected Holmes* (St. Martin's), edited by Marvin Kaye, a collection of double-pastiches based on the delightful premise that other famous writers (some within but most outside the detective fiction genre) were assigned to write Sherlock Holmes stories based on Watson's notes. Among the contributing authors (with their secondary literary targets in parentheses) are Henry Slesar (W. Somerset Maugham), Peter Cannon (C. S. Forester), Craig Shaw Gardner (Edgar Rice Burroughs), Mike Resnick (J. Thorne Smith), Richard A. Lupoff (Jack Kerouac), Edward D. Hoch (Ellery Queen), William L. DeAndrea (Mickey Spillane), and editor Kaye (Rex Stout).

The year also saw two of the best novel-length pastiches I can remember, both involving the Baker Street sleuth with real-life events: William Seil's *Sherlock Holmes and the Titanic Tragedy* (Breese), in which American mystery-writing great and *Titanic* victim Jacques Futrelle plays a prominent role, and Larry Millett's *Sherlock Holmes and the Red Demon* (Viking), a fair-play puzzle that brings Holmes and Watson to 1894 Minnesota to foil an arsonist.

It was also a great year for mystery fans at the movies. Three of the independent films that attracted so much attention at the Oscar ceremony may rank as cinematic crime classics in the years to come: Billy Bob Thornton's Edgar-winning *Sling Blade*, Joel & Ethan Coen's *Fargo*, and John Sayles's *Lone Star*.

In the world of mystery publishing, there are always murmurings of a shakeout and reduced lists, but you can't prove it by the numbers: 370 new hardcover novels were submitted for the 1996 Edgar award. Add all the firsts and paperback originals, and it's conservative to estimate another year of 500-plus new books.

BEST NOVELS OF THE YEAR 1996

For the second year out of three, I had the honor of chairing the committee to select the Edgar winner for best hardcover novel. This time, the committee got a late start, giving me an excuse to try out a method of operating the committee that I had proposed to MWA a decade ago but, to my knowledge, had never been tried. I assigned each committee member (myself, Ed Gorman, Kathleen Gregory Klein, Dick Lochte, and Margaret Maron) a specialized area of books from which to make recommendations, meaning that each member was expected not to read or extensively sample *all* of the 370 submitted books but about one-fifth of them, plus whatever titles the other panelists recommended as being potential nominees. Of course, we all received all the books and were free to range outside our areas of specialization as much as we desired. Given such a conscientious committee with such broad tastes, I think the system not only resulted in a first-rate short list of Edgar nominees but helped me make my own list of the fifteen best of the year easier to compile and maybe more authoritative.

With an added caveat that the following represent my views, not the committee's, here are my top fifteen for 1996:

Jay Brandon, *Defiance County* (Pocket). One of the most accomplished of the lawyer-novelists produces possibly his best book to date.

Max Allan Collins, *Damned in Paradise* (Dutton). Private eye Nate Heller helps out Clarence Darrow on Hawaii's notorious Massie rape-and-murder case in a far better fictionalization than Norman Katkov's famous *Blood and Orchids* (1983).

Thomas H. Cook, *The Chatham School Affair* (Bantam). The Edgar winner spans several decades in a memory piece that combines devious plotting (reader-as-detective) with evocatively elegiac prose. (Note: If I had managed to read it before last year's deadline, Cook's similarly structured *Breakheart Hill* would have been on my best-of-1995 list.)

Ed Gorman, *Cage of Night* (White Wolf). The master of dark suspense introduces a small-town outsider back from the service, a formerly unattainable homecoming queen, and possible extraterrestrials in one of his most enthralling and unpredictable novels.

Donald Honig, *The Sword of General Englund* (Scribners). No one who loves both westerns (particularly John Ford's cinematic U.S. Cavalry trilogy) and solid formal detective stories could resist this terrific novel of murder in 1870s Dakota Territory.

Stuart M. Kaminsky, *Blood and Rubles* (Fawcett Columbine). Moscow cop Porfiry Petrovich Rostnikov and his colleagues confront a variety of crimes in the troubled world of post-Soviet Russia, a changing background that only increases the appeal of this always fascinating series.

Margaret Lawrence, *Hearts and Bones* (Avon). The rich possibilities of combining American history and detection are further explored in the first novel, set in 1786, about Maine midwife and feminist-before-her-time Hannah Trevor.

Richard A. Lupoff, *The Silver Chariot Killer* (St. Martin's). Julius Caesar's toy chariot is the macguffin in the latest (and possibly best) of the continually diverting present-set-but-past-obsessed series about insurance investigator Hobart Lindsey (this time without his usual detective partner, Marvia Plum).

Sharyn McCrumb, *The Rosewood Casket* (Dutton). The author's Appalachian series, of which this is the fourth, seems to grow more impressive with each novel.

Michael Nava, *The Death of Friends* (Putnam). Chicano lawyer Henry Rios, here defending a friend on a murder charge, holds high rank among legal sleuths, ethnic sleuths, gay male sleuths, and most important, fully *human* sleuths.

Anne Perry, *Pentecost Alley* (Fawcett Columbine). Only a couple of years after Jack the Ripper, Charlotte and Thomas Pitt encounter another serial killer of London prostitutes in one of the high points of an incomparable series.

Peter Robinson, *Innocent Graves* (Berkley). Yorkshire's Alan Banks, a police detective in the league of P. D. James's Dalgliesh and Ruth Rendell's Wexford, searches for the killer of a child.

Steven Saylor, *A Murder on the Appian Way* (St. Martin's). Roman detective Gordianus the Finder appears for the fifth time (at book length) in one of the finest historical mystery series ever written.

Scott Turow, *The Laws of Our Fathers* (Farrar, Straus, Giroux). Though he may not sell quite as many copies as Grisham, the author of *Presumed Innocent* is without question the best of the lawyer-novelists to emerge in the last decade or two, as shown by this saga, covering three decades of American life, that is also, among other things, a detective story.

Carolyn Wheat, *Mean Streak* (Berkley). The fourth novel about lawyer Cass Jameson finds her wrestling with problems of legal ethics when asked to defend a former lover on federal corruption charges.

SHORT STORIES

As long as Douglas G. Greene's Crippen & Landru is in business, there will be hope for the single-author short story collection. The 1996 offerings from this admirable small press were the first collection of Edward D. Hoch's Dr. Sam Hawthorne impossible-crime stories, *Diagnosis: Impossible*; the latest of several collections of Bill Pronzini's Nameless Detective stories, *Spadework*; and the first gathering of Patricia Moyes's short fiction, *Who Killed Father Christmas? and Other Unseasonable Demises*. All three are available in both trade paperback editions and signed limited hardcovers (Crippen & Landru, P.O. Box 9315, Norfolk, VA 23505-9315).

Other small presses weighed in with notable single-author collections. Fedogan & Bremer (4325 Hiawatha Ave. #2115, Minneapolis, MN 55406) published handsome editions of obscure but talented pulp writer Howard

Wandrei's *The Last Pin* and Richard A. Lupoff's mixed collection *Before ... 12:01 ... and After*. The Metropolitan Toronto Reference Library's continuing Vincent Starrett Memorial Library series brought forth a third collection of the legendary Sherlockian's short detective stories, *The Memoirs of Jimmie Lavender* (order from The Battered Silicon Dispatch Box, P.O. Box 204, Shelburne, Ontario, Canada LON 1S0); and Gauntlet Publications (309 Powell Street, Springfield, PA 19064) produced Richard T. Chizmar's book of dark suspense tales, *Midnight Promises*. One of the best collections of the year came from a university press, the late John F. Suter's *Old Land, Dark Land, Strange Land* (University of Charleston, 2300 MacCorkle Ave., S. E., Charleston, WV 25304), while the "majors" came through with Robert Barnard's *The Habit of Widowhood* (Scribners), Ed Gorman's *Moonchasers and Other Stories* (Forge) and Mary Higgins Clark's *My Gal Sunday* (Simon & Schuster).

As for the multiauthor anthology market, there were again a large number of original-story gatherings, some restricted to one gender only (Barbara Collins and Robert J. Randisi's *Lethal Ladies* [Berkley], Sara Paretsky's *Women on the Case* [Delacorte]) but most democratically open to both: James Grady's *Unusual Suspects* (Vintage/Black Lizard), Otto Penzler's *Murder for Love* (Delacorte), the anonymously-edited *Malice Domestic 5* (Pocket), and Scott Turow's Mystery Writers of America anthology *Guilty as Charged* (Pocket).

Perhaps the most notable reprint anthology of the year was Tony Hillerman and Rosemary Herbert's *Oxford Book of American Detective Stories* (Oxford University Press). Also of value were Janet Hutchings's well-annotated gatherings from *Ellery Queen's Mystery Magazine, Once Upon a Crime II* and *Murder Most British* (both St. Martin's). The backfiles of *EQMM* and *Alfred Hitchcock's Mystery Magazine* produced several other theme anthologies edited by Cynthia Manson, either alone (*Garden of Deadly Delights* [Signet], *Mysterious Menagerie* [Berkley], and *Christmas Crimes* [Signet]), with Constance Scarborough (*Senior Sleuths* [Berkley] and *Win, Lose, or Die* [Carroll & Graf]), or with Kathleen Halligan (*Murder Intercontinental* [Carroll & Graf]). Robert J. Randisi edited *First Cases: The Private Eyes* (Dutton), while Charles G. Waugh and Martin H. Greenberg gathered *Supernatural Sleuths* (ROC).

More and more good anthologies are to be found on the instant-remainder tables of your local bookstore, most previously published, but some original. See, for example, Peter Haining's *London After Midnight* (Barnes & Noble); Ed Gorman, Larry Segriff, and Martin H. Greenberg's *Murder Most Irish* (Barnes & Noble); and the first volume in a planned decade-by-decade series, Marcia Muller and Bill Pronzini's *A Century of Mystery 1980–1989* (MJF Books).

REFERENCE BOOKS AND SECONDARY SOURCES

The major reference book event of the year was the publication of the *St. James Guide to Crime & Mystery Writers* (St. James/Gale), fourth edition of the source formerly known as *Twentieth-Century Crime and Mystery Writers*. With Jay P. Pederson taking the editorial helm, the massive 1264-page volume continues to be a prime source for biographical, bibliographic, and critical material on some 650 writers past and present, but the high incidence of errors caused considerable grumbling among knowledgable users.

Another useful reference source, Willetta L. Heising's Edgar-nominated *Detecting Women 2: A Reader's Guide and Checklist for Mystery Series Written by Women* (Purple Moon), will be followed in 1997 by the same author's *Detecting Men*.

My favorite secondary sources of the year were Malcolm J. Turnbull's *Elusion Aforethought: The Life and Writing of Anthony Berkeley Cox* (Bowling Green University Popular Press), the first book-length consideration of a relatively neglected figure (variously known as Anthony Berkeley, A. B. Cox, and Francis Iles) who is arguably as significant in detective fiction history as Christie or Sayers; and John J. Walsdorf's *Julian Symons: A Bibliography* (Oak Knoll), which includes considerable previously unpublished commentary by its subject. A worthy technical manual, both for its instructional and entertainment value, is Larry Beinhart's *How to Write a Mystery* (Ballantine).

SUBGENRES

I. Private Eyes. Among the sleuths-for-hire in entertaining form were Robert Crais's Elvis Cole in *Sunset Express* (Hyperion); Parnell Hall's Stanley Hastings in *Trial* (Mysterious), which can also be recommended for Perry Mason fans; Marcia Muller's Sharon McCone in *The Broken Promise Land* (Mysterious); Bill Pronzini's Nameless in *Sentinels* (Carroll & Graf); Sandra West Prowell's Phoebe Siegel in *When Wallflowers Die* (Walker); Sandra Scoppettone's Lauren Laurano in *Let's Face the Music and Die* (Little Brown); and John Lutz's Fred Carver in *Lightning* (Holt), which makes use of the ongoing abortion controversy in a way that will make neither side totally comfortable.

II. Formal Detection. Among the key titles for Golden-Age purists were Francis M. Nevins's *Into the Same River Twice* (Carroll & Graf), which shows a strong influence of Ellery Queen (along with Cornell Woolrich and

Erle Stanley Gardner); Peter Lovesey's *Bloodhounds* (Mysterious), concerning a locked-boat murder with a club of mystery readers as suspects; Nevada Barr's *Firestorm* (Putnam), a new variation on the closed-circle whodunit where the suspects are united in danger; and Michael Bowen's *Worst Case Scenario* (Crown), which features a locked room in the John Dickson Carr manner. Other classical sleuths in solid form included Margaret Maron's Judge Deborah Knott in *Up Jumps the Devil* (Mysterious) and David Handler's professional ghostwriter Stewart Hoag in *The Girl Who Ran Off With Daddy* (Doubleday). Sadly, two outstanding classical amateur detectives whose creators have died may have appeared for the last time, though we may hope for some posthumous publications: William L. DeAndrea's Matt Cobb in *Killed in the Fog* (Simon & Schuster) and Harry Kemelman's Rabbi David Small in *That Day the Rabbi Left Town* (Fawcett Columbine).

   III. Police procedurals. Working on this year's introduction always gives me a chance to tardily spot the errors in last year's; this time, I discovered I had jumped the gun and put an early 1996 book, Susan Dunlap's *Sudden Exposure* (Delacorte), on my list of the best of 1995. The good news is that I have an excuse to plug Berkeley cop Jill Smith's latest case two years in a row. Another formidable policewoman, Katherine V. Forrest's Kate Delafield, appears in the haunting *Liberty Square* (Berkley), about a reunion of Vietnam Marine Corps colleagues. The pseudonymous Robert Leigh builds up to a terrific surprise twist in the New York procedural *The Turner Journals* (Walker). Series cops in good form included Bill Crider's Sheriff Dan Rhodes in *Winning Can Be Murder* (St. Martin's); Janwillem van de Wetering's Amsterdam crew in *The Hollow-Eyed Angel* (Soho); and Tony Hillerman's Joe Leaphorn and Jim Chee in *The Fallen Man* (HarperCollins).

   IV. Historicals. It was another extraordinary year in this growing subgenre, which produced three of the five Edgar nominees (by Cook, Lawrence, and Perry) and three other titles on my list of fifteen. More and more writers are using a twentieth-century historical background. For example, J. Madison Davis's *And the Angels Sing* (Permanent) makes vivid use of the World War II–era big band and Army camp scene; and the Hollywood of years gone by was exploited once again (with celebrity guest stars) by George Baxt in *The William Powell/Myrna Loy Murder Case* (St. Martin's) and Stuart M. Kaminsky in *Dancing in the Dark* (Mysterious), featuring Fred Astaire. William F. Nolan's *The Marble Orchard* (St. Martin's) continued his fictionalization of a 1930s Chandler-Hammett-Gardner detecting team, this time with Chandler in the spotlight.

   Moving farther into the past, a famous composer serves as sleuth, as well as music tutor, to not-yet-Queen Victoria, in *Too Many Notes, Mr. Mozart* (Carroll & Graf) by Robert Barnard writing as Bernard Bastable. Other good historicals took us to mid-nineteenth-century upstate New York: Miriam Grace Monfredo's *Through a Glass Eagle* (Berkley); London of the same period: Anne Perry's *Weighed in the Balance* (Fawcett Columbine), from her secondary series about amnesiac detective William Monk and company; New York in 1895: Maan Meyers's *The House on Mulberry Street* (Bantam); the same city two decades earlier: J. D. Christilian's *Scarlet Women* (Fine) (the byline is one of many pseudonyms of the late Marvin H. Albert); and the traveling theatrical world of ancient Rome: Lindsey Davis's *Last Act in Palmyra* (Mysterious). Ed Gorman's *Hawk Moon* (St. Martin's) brings back his turn-of-the-century Iowa policewoman Anna Tolan, who alternates with present-day private eye Robert Payne in an interesting structural experiment. And finally, you may ask, how many appearances did P. C. Doherty (aka Paul Harding, C. L. Grace, Michael Clynes, Ann Dukthas) make during 1996? *At least* six, but it's hard to keep track. For a good example of his work, try Grace's *The Book of Shadows* (St. Martin's), a Carrian locked-room puzzle from the series about fifteenth-century physician Kathryn Swinbrooke.

V. **The Lawyers.** John Grisham's annual bestseller was *The Runaway Jury* (Doubleday), which may have been weak in the characterization department but certainly delivered a complex and devious (okay, and only marginally believable) plot concerning jury-tampering in a tobacco liability trial. Other lawyer-authors in good form included Barbara Parker with *Blood Relations* (Dutton), Robert K. Tanenbaum with *Falsely Accused* (Dutton), Lisa Scottoline with *Legal Tender* (HarperCollins), Philip Friedman with *Grand Jury* (Fine), William Bernhardt with *Cruel Justice* (Ballantine), and Paul Levine with *Fool Me Twice* (Morrow). Three lawyer sleuths from nonlawyer writers also had good 1996 cases: Ed McBain's Matthew Hope in *Gladly, the Cross-Eyed Bear* (Warner), Kate Wilhelm's Barbara Holloway in *Malice Prepense* (St. Martin's), and William G. Tapply's Brady Coyne in *Close to the Bone* (St. Martin's).

VI. **Thrillers.** Dean Koontz's *Intensity* (Knopf) was a notable example of pure suspense and menace, as was R. D. Zimmerman's Edgar-nominated paperback *Tribe* (Dell). Val Davis's *Track of the Scorpion* (St. Martin's) proved a fine beginning to a new aviation archaeology series, the unfamiliar byline concealing (but not for long) veteran novelist Robert Irvine and wife Angie; Gayle Lynds's *Masquerade* (Doubleday) marked the author a formidable new player in the international intrigue and espionage league; and Dick Francis's *To the Hilt* (Putnam), though not quite up to his best form, seemed to me a better book than his 1995 Edgar winner, *Come to Grief*.

OTHERS MENTIONED IN DISPATCHES

Have we mentioned all the major names to have new novels in 1996? Hardly. Also in the lists were Rita Mae Brown, Edna Buchanan, James Lee Burke, Robert Campbell, Mary Higgins Clark, Michael Connelly, K. C. Constantine, Patricia Cornwell, James Crumley, Len Deighton, Ken Follett, Frederick Forsyth, Nicolas Freeling, Elizabeth George, Joe Gores, Sue Grafton, Evan Hunter, Faye Kellerman, Jonathan Kellerman, Emma Lathen, Elmore Leonard, Charlotte MacLeod, Walter Mosley, Robert B. Parker, T. Jefferson Parker, Julie Smith, Martin Cruz Smith, Mickey Spillane, Minette Walters, Joseph Wambaugh, and Donald E. Westlake.

AWARD WINNERS FOR 1996

EDGAR ALLAN POE AWARDS
(Mystery Writers of America)

Best novel: Thomas H. Cook, *The Chatham School Affair* (Bantam)

Best first novel by an American author: John Morgan Wilson, *Simple Justice* (Doubleday)

Best original paperback: Harlan Coben, *Fadeaway* (Dell)

Best fact crime book: Darcy O'Brien, *Power to Hurt* (HarperCollins)

Best critical/biographical work: Michael Atkinson, *The Secret Marriage of Sherlock Holmes* (University of Michigan Press)

Best short story: Michael Malone, "Red Clay" (*Murder for Love* [Delacorte])

Best young adult mystery: Willo Davis Roberts, *Twisted Summer* (Atheneum)

Best juvenile mystery: Dorothy Reynolds Miller, *The Clearing* (Atheneum)

Best episode in a television series: Ed Zuckerman and I. C. Rapoport (*Law & Order*/NBC)

Best television feature or miniseries: Jimmy McGovern, "Brotherly Love" (*Cracker*/A&E)

Best motion picture: Billy Bob Thornton, *Sling Blade* (Miramax)

Grand master: Ruth Rendell

Robert L. Fish award (best first story): David Vaughn, "The Prosecutor of DuPrey" (*EQMM*, January)

Ellery Queen award: Francois Guerif
Raven: Marvin Lachman

AGATHA AWARDS
(Malice Domestic Mystery Convention)

Best novel: Margaret Maron, *Up Jumps the Devil* (Mysterious)
Best first novel: Anne George, *Murder on a Girl's Night Out*
Best short story: Carolyn Wheat, "Accidents Will Happen" (*Malice Domestic 5* [Pocket])
Best nonfiction: Willetta L. Heising, *Detecting Women 2* (Purple Moon)
Lifetime achievement: Emma Lathen

HAMMETT PRIZE
(North American Branch, International Association of Crime Writers)

Martin Cruz Smith, *Rose* (Random House)

AWARD WINNERS FOR 1995

ANTHONY AWARDS
(Bouchercon World Mystery Convention)

Best novel: Mary Willis Walker, *Under the Beetle's Cellar* (Doubleday)
Best first novel: Virginia Lanier, *Death in Bloodhound Red* (Pineapple)
Best paperback original: Harlan Coben, *Deal Breaker* (Dell)
Best true crime: Ann Rule, *Dead by Sunset* (Simon & Schuster)
Best short story: Gar Anthony Haywood, "And Pray Nobody Sees You" (*Spooks, Spies & Private Eyes* [Doubleday])
Best anthology or short story collection: Marcia Muller, *The McCone Files* (Crippen & Landru)
Best critical work: Kate Stine, ed., *The Armchair Detective Book of Lists*, 2nd edition (Penzler)
Best film: *The Usual Suspects*
Best TV series: *The X-Files*
Best Magazine/Digest/Review Publication: *The Armchair Detective*
Best Publisher: St. Martin's
Best Editor: Sara Ann Freed (Mysterious)
Best Cover Art: *The Body in the Transept* by Jeanne Dams (Walker)

SHAMUS AWARDS
(Private Eye Writers of America)

Best novel: S. J. Rozan, *Concourse* (St. Martin's)
  Best first novel: Richard Barre, *The Innocents* (Walker)
  Best original paperback novel: William Jaspersohn, *Native Angels* (Bantam)
  Best short story: Gar Anthony Haywood, "And Pray Nobody Sees You" (*Spooks, Spies & Private Eyes* [Doubleday])

DAGGER AWARDS
(Crime Writers' Association, Great Britain)

Gold Dagger: Ben Elton, *Popcorn*
  Silver Dagger: Peter Lovesey, *Bloodhound*
  John Creasey Award (Best First Novel): None awarded
  Best short story: Ian Rankin, "Herbert in Motion"
  Best nonfiction: Antonia Fraser, *The Gunpowder Plot*
  Last Laugh: Janet Evanovich, *Two for the Dough*
  Dagger in the Library: Marion Babson
  Rusty Dagger: Dorothy L. Sayers, *The Nine Tailors*

MACAVITY AWARDS
(Mystery Readers International)

Best novel: Mary Willis Walker, *Under the Beetle's Cellar* (Doubleday)
  Best first novel: Dianne Day, *The Strange Files of Fremont Jones* (Doubleday)
  Best critical/biographical work: Willetta L. Heising, *Detecting Women* (Purple Moon)
  Best short story: Colin Dexter, "Evans Tries an O-Level" (*Morse's Greatest Mystery and Other Stories* (Crown)

ARTHUR ELLIS AWARDS
(Crime Writers of Canada)

Best novel: L. R. Wright, *Mother Love* (Doubleday)
  Best first novel: tie, D. H. Toole, *Moonlit Days and Nights* (Cormorant), and John Spencer Hill, *The Last Castrato* (Constable)
  Best nonfiction: Lois Simmie, *The Secret Lives of Sgt. John Wilson: A*

True Story of Love & Murder (Greystone)
 Best short story: Mary Jane Maffini, "Cotton Armour" (*The Ladies Killing Circle* [General Store])
 Best juvenile: Nora McClintock, *Mistaken Identity* (Scholastic)

HAMMETT PRIZE
(North American Branch, International Association of Crime Writers)

Mary Willis Walker, *Under the Beetle's Cellar* (Doubleday)

The following story is not Brendan Du Bois's first appearance in our annual collection. Last time it was with "The Necessary Brother" in *The Year's 25 Finest, 4th edition.* Here he weighs in with another tale of an outsider who is just trying to do what's right. In this case, it's enjoying his well-deserved retirement. Unfortunately, some locals just plain don't like newcomers. Set in the stark beauty of the New England hills, the opening lines of "The Dark Snow" will show why it was nominated for the 1996 Edgar Award.

The Dark Snow
BRENDAN DU BOIS

When I get to the steps of my lakeside home, the door is open. I slowly walk in, my hand reaching for the phantom weapon at my side, everything about me extended and tingling as I enter the strange place that used to be mine. I step through the small kitchen, my boots crunching the broken glassware and dishes on the tile floor. Inside the living room with its cathedral ceiling the furniture has been upended, as if an earthquake had struck.

I pause for a second, looking out the large windows and past the enclosed porch, down to the frozen waters of Lake Marie. Off in the distance are the snow-covered peaks of the White Mountains. I wait, trembling, my hand still curving for that elusive weapon. They are gone, but their handiwork remains. The living room is a jumble of furniture, torn books and magazines, shattered pictures and frames. On one clear white plaster wall, next to the fireplace, two words have been written in what looks to be ketchup: GO HOME.

This is my home. I turn over a chair and drag it to the windows. I sit and look out at the crisp winter landscape, my legs stretched out, holding both hands still in my lap, which is quite a feat.

For my hands at that moment want to be wrapped around someone's throat.

AFTER A LONG TIME WANDERING, I came to Nansen, New Hampshire in the late summer and purchased a house along the shoreline of Lake Marie.

1

I didn't waste much time, and I didn't bargain. I made an offer that was about a thousand dollars below the asking price, and in less than a month it belonged to me.

At first I didn't know what to do with it. I had never had a residence that was actually mine. Everything before this had been apartments, hotel rooms or temporary officer's quarters. The first few nights I couldn't sleep inside. I would go outside to the long dock that extends into the deep blue waters of the lake, bundle myself up in a sleeping bag over a thin foam mattress and stare up at the stars, listening to the loons getting ready for their long winter trip. The loons don't necessarily fly south; the ones here go out to the cold Atlantic and float with the waves and currents, not once touching land the entire winter.

As I snuggled in my bag I thought it was a good analogy for what I'd been doing. I had drifted too long. It was time to come back to dry land.

AFTER GETTING THE POWER AND other utilities up and running and moving in the few boxes of stuff that belonged to me, I checked the bulky folder that had accompanied my retirement and pulled out an envelope with a doctor's name on it. Inside were official papers that directed me to talk to him, and I shrugged and decided it was better than sitting in an empty house getting drunk. I phoned and got an appointment for the next day.

His name was Ron Longley and he worked in Manchester, the state's largest city and about an hour's drive south of Lake Marie. His office was in a refurbished brick building along the banks of the Merrimack River. I imagined I could still smell the sweat and toil of the French Canadians who had worked here for so many years in the shoe, textile and leather mills until their distant cousins in Georgia and Alabama took their jobs away.

I wasn't too sure what to make of Ron during our first session. He showed me some documents that made him a Department of Defense contractor and gave his current classification level, and then, after signing the usual insurance nonsense, we got down to it. He was about ten years younger than I, with a mustache and not much hair on top. He wore jeans, a light blue shirt and a tie that looked as if about six tubes of paint had been squirted onto it, and he said, "Well, here we are."

"That we are," I said. "And would you believe I've already forgotten if you're a psychologist or a psychiatrist?"

That made for a good laugh. With a casual wave of his hand, he said, "Makes no difference. What would you like to talk about?"

"What should I talk about?"

A shrug, one of many I would eventually see. "Whatever's on your mind."

"Really?" I said, not bothering to hide the challenge in my voice. "Try this one on then, doc. I'm wondering what I'm doing here. And another thing I'm wondering about is paperwork. Are you going to be making a report down south on how I do? You working under some deadline, some pressure?"

His hands were on his belly and he smiled. "Nope."

"Not at all?"

"Not at all," he said. "If you want to come in here and talk baseball for 50 minutes, that's fine with me."

I looked at him and those eyes. Maybe it's my change of view since retirement, but there was something trustworthy about him. I said, "You know what's really on my mind?"

"No, but I'd like to know."

"My new house," I said. "It's great. It's on a big lake and there aren't any close neighbors, and I can sit on the dock at night and see stars I haven't seen in a long time. But I've been having problems sleeping."

"Why's that?" he asked, and I was glad he wasn't one of those stereo-typical head docs, the ones who take a lot of notes.

"Weapons."

"Weapons?"

I nodded. "Yeah, I miss my weapons." A deep breath. "Look, you've seen my files, you know the places Uncle Sam has sent me and the jobs I've done. All those years, I had pistols or rifles or heavy weapons, always at my side, under my bed or in a closet. But when I moved into that house, well, I don't have them anymore."

"How does that make you feel?" Even though the question was friendly, I knew it was a real doc question and not a from-the-next-barstool type of question.

I rubbed my hands. "I really feel like I'm changing my ways. But damn it. . . ."

"Yes?"

I smiled. "I sure could use a good night's sleep."

As I DROVE BACK HOME, I thought, Hell, it's only a little white lie.

The fact is, I did have my weapons.

They were locked up in the basement, in strongboxes with heavy combination locks. I couldn't get to them quickly, but I certainly hadn't tossed them away.

I hadn't been lying when I told Ron I couldn't sleep. That part was entirely true.

I thought, as I drove up the dirt road to my house, scaring a possum that scuttled along the side of the gravel, that the real problem with living in my new home was so slight that I was embarrassed to bring it up to Ron.

It was the noise.

*   *   *

I WAS LIVING IN A rural paradise, with clean air, clean water and views of the woods and lake and mountains that almost broke my heart each time I climbed out of bed, stiff with old dreams and old scars. The long days were filled with work and activities I'd never had time for. Cutting old brush and trimming dead branches. Planting annuals. Clearing my tiny beach of leaves and other debris. Filling bird feeders. And during the long evenings on the front porch or on the dock, I tackled thick history books.

But one night after dinner—I surprised myself at how much I enjoyed cooking—I was out on the dock, sitting in a Fifties-era web lawn chair, a glass of red wine in my hand and a history of the Apollo space program in my lap. Along the shoreline of Lake Marie, I could see the lights of the cottages and other homes. Every night there were fewer and fewer lights, as more of the summer people boarded up their places and headed back to suburbia.

I was enjoying my wine and the book and the slight breeze, but there was also a distraction: three high-powered speedboats, racing around on the lake and tossing up great spray and noise. They were dragging people along in inner tubes, and it was hard to concentrate on my book. After a while the engines slowed and I was hoping the boats would head back to their docks, but they drifted together and ropes were exchanged, and soon they became a large raft. A couple of grills were set up and there were more hoots and yells, and then a sound system kicked in, with rock music and a heavy bass that echoed among the hills.

It was then too dark to read and I'd lost interest in the wine. I was sitting there, arms folded tight against my chest, trying hard to breathe. The noise got louder and I gave up and retreated into the house, where the heavy thump-thump of the bass followed me in. If I'd had a boat I could have gone out and asked them politely to turn it down, but that would have meant talking with people and putting myself in the way, and I didn't want to do that.

Instead, I went upstairs to my bedroom and shut the door and windows. Still, that thump-thump shook the beams of the house. I lay down with a pillow wrapped about my head and tried not to think of what was in the basement.

LATER THAT NIGHT I GOT up for a drink of water, and there was still noise and music. I walked out onto the porch and could see movement on the lake and hear laughter. On a tree near the dock was a spotlight that the previous owners had installed and which I had rarely used. I flipped on the switch. Some shouts and shrieks. Two powerboats, tied together, had drifted close to my shore. The light caught a young muscular man with a fierce black mustache standing on the stern of his powerboat and urinating into the lake. His half a dozen companions, male and female, yelled and cursed in my direction. The boats started up and two men and a young woman stumbled to the side of one and dropped their bathing suits, exposing their buttocks. A couple others gave me a one-fingered salute, and there was a shower of bottles and cans tossed over the side as they sped away.

I spent the next hour on the porch, staring into the darkness.

THE NEXT DAY I MADE two phone calls, to the town hall and the police department of Nansen. I made gentle and polite inquiries and got the same answers from each office. There was no local or state law about boats coming to within a certain distance of shore. There was no law forbidding boats from mooring together. Nansen being such a small town, there was also no noise ordinance.

Home sweet home.

ON MY NEXT VISIT RON was wearing a bow tie, and we discussed necktie fashions before we got into the business at hand. He said, "Still having sleeping problems?"

I smiled. "No, not at all."

"Really?"

"It's fall," I said. "The tourists have gone home, most of the cottages along the lake have been boarded up and nobody takes out boats anymore. It's so quiet at night I can hear the house creak and settle."

"That's good, that's really good," Ron said, and I changed the subject. A half hour later, I was heading back to Nansen, thinking about my latest white lie. Well, it wasn't really a lie. More of an oversight.

I hadn't told Ron about the hang-up phone calls. Or how trash had twice been dumped in my driveway. Or how a week ago, when I was shopping, I had come back to find a bullet hole through one of my windows. Maybe it had been a hunting accident. Hunting season hadn't started, but I knew that for some of the workingmen in this town, it didn't matter when the state allowed them to do their shooting.

I had cleaned up the driveway, shrugged off the phone calls and cut away brush and saplings around the house, to eliminate any hiding spots for . . . hunters.

Still, I could sit out on the dock, a blanket around my legs and a mug of tea in my hand, watching the sun set in the distance, the reddish pink highlighting the strong yellows, oranges and reds of the fall foliage. The water was a slate gray, and though I missed the loons, the smell of the leaves and the tang of woodsmoke from my chimney seemed to settle in just fine.

* * *

AS IT GREW COLDER, I began to go into town for breakfast every few days. The center of Nansen could be featured in a documentary on New Hampshire small towns. Around the green common with its Civil War statue are a bank, a real estate office, a hardware store, two gas stations, a general store and a small strip of service places with everything from a plumber to video rentals and Gretchen's Kitchen. At Gretchen's I read the paper while letting the mornings drift by. I listened to the old-timers at the counter pontificate on the ills of the state, nation and world, and watched harried workers fly in to grab a quick meal. Eventually, a waitress named Sandy took some interest in me.

She was about 20 years younger than I, with raven hair, a wide smile and a pleasing body that filled out her regulation pink uniform. After a couple weeks of flirting and generous tips on my part, I asked her out, and when she said yes, I went to my pickup truck and burst out laughing. A real date. I couldn't remember the last time I had had a real date.

The first date was dinner a couple of towns over, in Montcalm, the second was dinner and a movie outside Manchester and the third was dinner at my house, which was supposed to end with a rented movie in the living room but instead ended up in the bedroom. Along the way I learned that Sandy had always lived in Nansen, was divorced with two young boys and was saving her money so she could go back to school and become a legal aide. "If you think I'm going to keep slinging hash and waiting for Billy to send his support check, then you're a damn fool," she said on our first date.

After a bedroom interlude that surprised me with its intensity, we sat on the enclosed porch. I opened a window for Sandy, who needed a smoke. The house was warm and I had on a pair of shorts; she had wrapped a towel around her torso. I sprawled in an easy chair while she sat on the couch, feet in my lap. Both of us had glasses of wine and I felt comfortable and tingling. Sandy glanced at me as she worked on her cigarette. I'd left the lights off and lit a couple of candles, and in the hazy yellow light, I could see the small tattoo of a unicorn on her right shoulder.

Sandy looked at me and asked, "What were you doing when you was in the government?"

"Traveled a lot and ate bad food."

"No, really," she said. "I want a straight answer."

Well, I thought, as straight as I can be. I said, "I was a consultant, to foreign armies. Sometimes they needed help with certain weapons or training techniques. That was my job."

"Were you good?"

Too good, I thought. "I did all right."

"You've got a few scars there."

"That I do."

She shrugged, took a lazy puff off her cigarette. "I've seen worse."

I wasn't sure where this was headed. Then she said, "When are you going to be leaving?"

Confused, I asked her, "You mean, tonight?"

"No," she said. "I mean, when are you leaving Nansen and going back home?"

I looked around the porch and said, "This is my home."

She gave me a slight smile, like a teacher correcting a fumbling but eager student. "No, it's not. This place was built by the Gerrish family. It's the Gerrish place. You're from away, and this ain't your home."

I tried to smile, though my mood was slipping. "Well, I beg to disagree."

She said nothing for a moment, just studied the trail of smoke from her cigarette. Then she said, "Some people in town don't like you. They think you're uppity, a guy that don't belong here."

I began to find it quite cool on the porch. "What kind of people?"

"The Garr brothers. Jerry Tompkins. Kit Broderick. A few others. Guys in town. They don't particularly like you."

"I don't particularly care," I shot back.

A small shrug as she stubbed out her cigarette. "You will."

The night crumbled some more after that, and the next morning, while sitting in the corner at Gretchen's, I was ignored by Sandy. One of the older waitresses served me, and my coffee arrived in a cup stained with lipstick, the bacon was charred black and the eggs were cold. I got the message. I started making breakfast at home, sitting alone on the porch, watching the leaves fall and days grow shorter.

I wondered if Sandy was on her own or if she had been scouting out enemy territory on someone's behalf.

AT MY DECEMBER VISIT, I surprised myself by telling Ron about something that had been bothering me.

"It's the snow," I said, leaning forward, hands clasped between my legs. "It's going to start snowing soon. And I've always hated the snow, especially since. . . ."

"Since when?"

"Since something I did once," I said. "In Serbia."

"Go on," he said, fingers making a tent in front of his face.

"I'm not sure I can."

Ron tilted his head quizzically. "You know I have the clearances."

I cleared my throat, my eyes burning a bit. "I know. It's just that it's. . . . Ever see blood on snow, at night?"

I had his attention. "No," he said, "no, I haven't."

"It steams at first, since it's so warm," I said. "And then it gets real dark, almost black. Dark snow, if you can believe it. It's something that stays with you, always."

He looked steadily at me for a moment, then said, "Do you want to talk about it some more?"

"No."

I SPENT ALL OF ONE gray afternoon in my office cubbyhole, trying to get a new computer up and running. When at last I went downstairs for a quick drink, I looked outside and there they were, big snowflakes lazily drifting to the ground. Forgetting about the drink, I went out to the porch and looked at the pure whiteness of everything, of the snow covering the bare limbs, the shrubbery and the frozen lake. I stood there and hugged myself, admiring the softly accumulating blanket of white and feeling lucky.

TWO DAYS AFTER THE SNOWSTORM I was out on the frozen waters of Lake Marie, breathing hard and sweating and enjoying every second of it. The day before I had driven into Manchester to a sporting goods store and had come out with a pair of cross-country skis. The air was crisp and still, and the sky was a blue so deep I half-expected to see brushstrokes. From the lake, I looked back at my home and liked what I saw. The white paint and plain construction made me smile for no particular reason. I heard not a single sound, except for the faint drone of a distant airplane. Before me someone had placed signs and orange ropes in the snow, covering an oval area at the center of the lake. Each sign said the same thing: DANGER! THIN ICE! I remembered the old-timers at Gretchen's Kitchen telling a story about a hidden spring coming up through the lake bottom, or some damn thing, that made ice at the center of the lake thin, even in the coldest weather. I got cold and it was time to go home.

About halfway back to the house is where it happened.

AT FIRST IT WAS A quiet sound, and I thought that it was another airplane. Then the noise got louder and louder, and separated, becoming distinct. Snowmobiles, several of them. I turned and they came speeding out of the woods, tossing up great rooster tails of snow and ice. They were headed straight for me. I turned away and kept up a steady pace, trying to ignore the growing loudness of the approaching engines. An itchy feeling crawled up my spine to the base of my head, and the noise exploded in pitch as they raced by me.

Even over the loudness of the engines I could make out the yells as the snowmobiles roared by, hurling snow in my direction. There were two people to each machine and they didn't look human. Each was dressed in a bulky jumpsuit, heavy boots and a padded helmet. They raced by and, sure enough, circled around and came back at me. This time I flinched. This time, too, a couple of empty beer cans were thrown my way.

By the third pass, I was getting closer to my house. I thought it was almost over when one of the snowmobiles broke free from the pack and raced across about 50 feet in front of me. The driver turned so that the machine was blocking me and sat there, racing the throttle. Then he pulled off his helmet, showing an angry face and thick mustache, and I recognized him as the man on the powerboat a few months earlier. He handed his helmet to his passenger, stepped off the snowmobile and unzipped his jumpsuit. It took only a moment as he marked the snow in a long, steaming stream, and there was laughter from the others as he got back on the machine and sped away. I skied over the soiled snow and took my time climbing up the snow-covered shore. I entered my home, carrying my skis and poles like weapons over my shoulder.

THAT NIGHT, AND EVERY NIGHT afterward, they came back, breaking the winter stillness with the throbbing sounds of engines, laughter, drunken shouts and music from portable stereos. Each morning I cleared away their debris and scuffed fresh snow over the stains. In the quiet of my house, I found myself constantly on edge, listening, waiting for the noise to suddenly return and break up the day. Phone calls to the police department and town hall confirmed what I already knew: Except for maybe littering, no ordinances or laws were being broken.

On one particularly loud night, I broke a promise to myself and went to the tiny, damp cellar to unlock the green metal case holding a pistol-shaped device. I went back upstairs to the enclosed porch, and with the lights off, I switched on the night-vision scope and looked at the scene below me. Six snowmobiles were parked in a circle on the snow-covered ice, and in the center, a fire had been made. Figures stumbled around in the snow, talking and laughing. Stereos had been set up on the seats of two of the snow-mobiles, and the loud music with its bass thump-thump-thump echoed across the flat ice. Lake Marie is one of the largest bodies of water in this part of the country, but the camp was set up right below my windows.

I watched for a while as they partied. Two of the black-suited figures started wrestling in the snow. More shouts and laughter, and then the fight broke up and someone turned the stereos even louder. Thump-thump-thump.

I switched off the nightscope, returned it to its case in the cellar and went to bed. Even with foam rubber plugs in my ears, the bass noise reverberated inside my skull. I put the pillow across my face and tried to ignore the sure knowledge that this would continue all winter, the noise and the littering and the aggravation, and when the spring came, they would turn in their snowmobiles for boats, and they'd be back, all summer long.

Thump-thump-thump.

AT THE NEXT SESSION WITH Ron, we talked about the weather until he pierced me with his gaze and said, "Tell me what's wrong."

I went through half a dozen rehearsals of what to tell him, and then skated to the edge of the truth and said, "I'm having a hard time adjusting, that's all."

"Adjusting to what?"

"To my home," I said, my hands clasped before me. "I never thought I would say this, but I'm really beginning to get settled, for the first time in my life. You ever been in the military, Ron?"

"No, but I know—"

I held up my hand. "Yes, I know what you're going to say. You've worked as a consultant, but you've never been one of us, Ron. Never. You can't know what it's like, constantly being ordered to uproot yourself and go halfway across the world to a new place with a different language, customs and weather, all within a week. You never settle in, never really get into a place you call home."

He swiveled a bit in his black leather chair, "But that's different now?"

"It sure is," I said.

There was a pause as we looked at each other, and Ron said, "But something is going on."

"Something is."

"Tell me."

And then I knew I wouldn't. A fire wall had already been set up between Ron and the details of what was going on back at my home. If I let him know what was really happening, I knew that he would make a report, and within the week I'd be ordered to go somewhere else. If I'd been younger and not so dependent on a monthly check, I would have put up a fight.

But now, no more fighting. I looked past Ron and said, "An adjustment problem, I guess."

"Adjusting to civilian life?"

"More than that," I said. "Adjusting to Nansen. It's a great little town, but . . . I feel like an outsider."

"That's to be expected."

"Sure, but I still don't like it. I know it will take some time, but . . . well, I get the odd looks, the quiet little comments, the cold shoulders."

Ron seemed to choose his words carefully. "Is that proving to be a serious problem?"

Not even a moment of hesitation as I lied: "No, not at all."

"And what do you plan on doing?"

An innocent shrug. "Not much. Just try to fit in, try to be a good neighbor."

"That's all?"

I nodded firmly. "That's all."

IT TOOK A BIT OF research, but eventually I managed to put a name to the face of the mustached man who had pissed on my territory. Jerry Tompkins. Floor supervisor for a computer firm outside Manchester, married with three kids, an avid boater, snowmobiler, hunter and all-around guy. His family had been in Nansen for generations, and his dad was one of the three selectmen who ran the town. Using a couple of old skills, I tracked him down one dark afternoon and pulled my truck next to his in the snowy parking lot of a tavern on the outskirts of Nansen. The tavern was called Peter's Pub and its windows were barred and blacked out.

I stepped out of my truck and called to him as he walked to the entrance of the pub. He turned and glared at me. "What?"

"You're Jerry Tompkins, aren't you."

"Sure am," he said, hands in the pockets of his dark-green parka. "And you're the fella that's living up in the old Gerrish place."

"Yes, and I'd like to talk with you for a second."

His face was rough, like he had spent a lot of time outdoors in the wind and rain and an equal amount indoors, with cigarette smoke and loud country music. He rocked back on his heels with a little smile and said, "Go ahead. You got your second."

"Thanks," I said. "Tell you what, Jerry, I'm looking for something."

"And what's that?"

"I'm looking for a treaty."

He nodded, squinting his eyes. "What kind of treaty?"

"A peace treaty. Let's cut out the snowmobile parties on the lake by my place and the trash dumped in the driveway and the hang-up calls. Let's start fresh and just stay out of each other's way. What do you say? Then, this summer, you can all come over to my place for a cookout. I'll even supply the beer."

He rubbed at the bristles along his chin. "Seems like a one-sided deal. Not too sure what I get out of it."

"What's the point in what you're doing now?"

A furtive smile. "It suits me."

I felt like I was beginning to lose it. "You agree with the treaty, we all win."

"Still don't see what I get out of it," he said.

"That's the purpose of a peace treaty," I said. "You get peace."

"Feel pretty peaceful right now."

"That might change," I said, instantly regretting the words.

His eyes darkened. "Are you threatening me?"

A retreat, recalling my promise to myself when I'd come here. "No, not a threat, Jerry. What do you say?"

He turned and walked away, moving his head to keep me in view. "Your second got used up a long time ago, pal. And you better be out of this lot in another minute, or I'm going inside and coming out with a bunch of my friends. You won't like that."

No, I wouldn't, and it wouldn't be for the reason Jerry believed. If they did come out I'd be forced into old habits and old actions, and I'd promised myself I wouldn't do that. I couldn't.

"You got it," I said, backing away. "But remember, Jerry. Always."

"What's that?"

"The peace treaty," I said, going to the door of my pickup truck. "I offered."

ANOTHER VISIT TO RON, ON a snowy day. The conversation meandered along, and I don't know what got into me, but I looked out the old mill windows and said, "What do people expect, anyway?"

"What do you mean?" he asked.

"You take a tough teenager from a small Ohio town, and you train him and train him and train him. You turn him into a very efficient hunter, a meat eater. Then, after 20 or 30 years, you say thank you very much and send him back to the world of quiet vegetarians, and you expect him to start eating cabbages and carrots with no fuss or muss. A hell of a thing, thinking you can expect him to put away his tools and skills."

"Maybe that's why we're here," he suggested.

"Oh, please," I said. "Do you think this makes a difference?"

"Does it make a difference to you?"

I kept looking out the window. "Too soon to tell, I'd say. Truth is, I wonder if this is meant to work, or is just meant to make some people feel less guilty. The people who did the hiring, training and discharging."

"What do you think?"

I turned to him. "I think for the amount of money you charge Uncle Sam, you ask too many damn questions."

ANOTHER NIGHT AT TWO A.M. I was back outside, beside the porch, again with the nightscope in my hands. They were back, and if anything, the music and the engines blared even louder. A fire burned merrily among the snowmobiles, and as the revelers pranced and hollered, I wondered if some base part of their brains was remembering thousand-year-old rituals. As I looked at their dancing and drinking figures, I kept thinking of the long case at the other end of the cellar. Nice heavy-duty assault rifle with another night-vision scope, this one with crosshairs. Scan and track. Put a crosshair across each one's chest. Feel the weight of a fully loaded clip in your hand. Know that with a silencer on the end of the rifle, you could quietly take out that crew in a fistful of seconds. Get your mind back into the realm of possibilities, of cartridges and windage and grains and velocities. How long could it take between the time you said go and the time you could say mission accomplished? Not long at all.

"No," I whispered, switching off the scope.

I stayed on the porch for another hour, and as my eyes adjusted, I saw more movements. I picked up the scope. A couple of snow machines moved in, each with shapes on the seats behind the drivers. They pulled up to the snowy bank and the people moved quickly, intent on their work. Trash bags were tossed on my land, about eight or nine, and to add a bit more fun, each bag had been slit several times with a knife so it could burst open and spew its contents when it hit the ground. A few more hoots and hollers and the snowmobiles growled away, leaving trash and the flickering fire behind. I watched the lights as the snowmobiles roared across the lake and finally disappeared, though their sound did not.

The nightscope went back onto my lap. The rifle, I thought, could have stopped the fun right there with a couple of rounds through the engines. Highly illegal, but it would get their attention, right?

Right.

IN MY NEXT SESSION WITH Ron, I got to the point. "What kind of reports are you sending south?"

I think I might have surprised him. "Reports?"

"How I'm adjusting, that sort of thing."

He paused for a moment, and I knew there must be a lot of figuring going on behind those smiling eyes. "Just the usual things, that's all. That you're doing fine."

"Am I?"

"Seems so to me."

"Good." I waited for a moment, letting the words twist about on my tongue. "Then you can send them this message. I haven't been a hundred percent with you during these sessions, Ron. Guess it's not in my nature to be so open. But you can count on this. I won't lose it. I won't go into a gun shop and then take down a bunch of civilians. I'm not going to start hanging around 1600 Pennsylvania Avenue. I'm going to be all right."

He smiled. "I have never had any doubt."

"Sure you've had doubts," I said, smiling back. "But it's awfully polite of you to say otherwise."

*   *   *

ON A BRIGHT SATURDAY, I tracked down the police chief of Nansen at one of the two service stations in town, Glen's Gas & Repair. His cruiser, ordinarily a dark blue, was now a ghostly shade of white from the salt used to keep the roads clear. I parked at the side of the garage, and walking by the service bays, I could sense that I was being watched. I saw three cars with their hoods up, and I also saw a familiar uniform: black snow-mobile jumpsuits.

The chief was overweight and wearing a heavy blue jacket with a black Navy watch cap. His face was open and friendly, and he nodded in all the right places as I told him my story.

"Not much I can do, I'm afraid," he said, leaning against the door of his cruiser, one of two in the entire town. "I'd have to catch 'em in the act of trashing your place, and that means surveillance, and that means over-time hours, which I don't have."

"Surveillance would be a waste of time anyway," I replied. "These guys, they aren't thugs, right? For lack of a better phrase, they're good old boys, and they know everything that's going on in Nansen, and they'd know if you were setting up surveillance. And then they wouldn't show."

"You might think you're insulting me, but you're not," he said gently. "That's just the way things are done here. It's a good town and most of us get along, and I'm not kept that busy, not at all."

"I appreciate that, but you should also appreciate my problem," I said. "I live here and pay taxes, and people are harassing me. I'm looking for some assistance, that's all, and a suggestion of what I can do."

"You could move," the chief said, raising his coffee cup.

"Hell of a suggestion."

"Best one I can come up with. Look, friend, you're new here, you've got no family, no ties. You're asking me to take on some prominent families just because you don't get along with them. So why don't you move on? Find someplace smaller, hell, even someplace bigger, where you don't stand out so much. But face it, it's not going to get any easier."

"Real nice folks," I said, letting an edge of bitterness into my voice.

That didn't seem to bother the chief. "That they are. They work hard and play hard, and they pay taxes, too, and they look out for one another. I know they look like hell-raisers to you, but they're more than that. They're part of the community. Why, just next week, a bunch of them are going on a midnight snow run across the lake and into the mountains, raising money for the children's camp up at Lake Montcalm. People who don't care wouldn't do that."

"I just wish they didn't care so much about me."

He shrugged and said, "Look, I'll see what I can do. . . ." but the tone of his voice made it clear he wasn't going to do a damn thing.

The chief clambered into his cruiser and drove off, and as I walked past the bays of the service station, I heard snickers. I went around to my pickup truck and saw the source of the merriment.

My truck was resting heavily on four flat tires.

AT NIGHT I WOKE UP from cold and bloody dreams and let my thoughts drift into fantasies. By now I knew who all of them were, where all of them lived. I could go to their houses, every one of them, and bring them back and bind them in the basement of my home. I could tell them who I was and what I've done and what I can do, and I would ask them to leave me alone. That's it. Just give me peace and solitude and everything will be all right.

And they would hear me out and nod and agree, but I would know that I had to convince them. So I would go to Jerry Tompkins, the mustached one who enjoyed marking my territory, and to make my point, break a couple of his fingers, the popping noise echoing in the dark confines of the tiny basement.

Nice fantasies.

I ASKED RON, "WHAT'S THE point?"

He was comfortable in his chair, hands clasped over his little potbelly. "I'm sorry?"

"The point of our sessions."

His eyes were unflinching. "To help you adjust."

"Adjust to what?"

"To civilian life."

I shifted on the couch. "Let me get this. I work my entire life for this country, doing service for its civilians. I expose myself to death and injury every week, earning about a third of what I could be making in the private sector. And when I'm through, I have to adjust, I have to make allowances for civilians. But civilians, they don't have to do a damn thing. Is that right?"

"I'm afraid so."

"Hell of a deal."

He continued a steady gaze. "Only one you've got."

So HERE I AM, IN the smelly rubble that used to be my home. I make a few halfhearted attempts to turn the furniture back over and do some cleanup work, but I'm not in the mood. Old feelings and emotions are coursing through me, taking control. I take a few deep breaths and then I'm in the cellar, switching on the single lightbulb that hangs down from the rafters by a frayed black cord. As I maneuver among the packing cases, undoing combination locks, my shoulder strikes the lightbulb, causing it to swing back and forth, casting crazy shadows on the stone walls.

The night air is cool and crisp, and I shuffle through the snow around the house as I load the pickup truck, making three trips in all. I drive under the speed limit and halt completely at all stop signs as I go through the center of town. I drive around, wasting minutes and hours, listening to the radio. This late at night and being so far north, a lot of the stations that I can pick up are from Quebec, and there's a joyous lilt to the French-Canadian music and words that makes something inside me ache with longing.

When it's almost a new day, I drive down a street called Mast Road. Most towns around here have a Mast Road, where colonial surveyors marked tall pines that would eventually become masts for the Royal Navy. Tonight there are no surveyors, just the night air and darkness and a skinny rabbit racing across the cracked asphalt. When I'm near the target, I switch off the lights and engine and let the truck glide the last few hundred feet or so. I pull up across from a darkened house. A pickup truck and a Subaru station wagon are in the driveway. Gray smoke is wafting up from the chimney.

I roll down the window, the cold air washing over me like a wave of water. I pause, remembering what has gone on these past weeks, and then I get to work.

The nightscope comes up and clicks into action, and the name on the mailbox is clear enough in the sharp green light. TOMPKINS, in silver and black stick-on letters. I scan the two-story Cape Cod, checking out the surroundings. There's an attached garage to the right and a sunroom to the left. There is a front door and two other doors in a breezeway that runs from the garage to the house. There are no rear doors.

I let the nightscope rest on my lap as I reach toward my weapons. The first is a grenade launcher, with a handful of white phosphorus rounds clustered on the seat next to it like a gathering of metal eggs. Next to the grenade launcher is a 9mm Uzi, with an extended wooden stock for easier use. Another night-vision scope with crosshairs is attached to the Uzi.

Another series of deep breaths. Easy enough plan. Pop a white phosphorus round into the breezeway and another into the sunroom. In a minute or two both ends of the house are on fire. Our snowmobiler friend and his family wake up and, groggy from sleep and the fire and the noise, stumble out the front door onto the snow-covered lawn.

With the Uzi in my hand and the crosshairs on a certain face, a face with a mustache, I take care of business and drive to the next house.

I pick up the grenade launcher and rest the barrel on the open window. It's cold. I rub my legs together and look outside at the stars. The wind comes up and snow blows across the road. I hear the low hoo-hoo-hoo of an owl.

I bring the grenade launcher up, resting the stock against my cheek. I aim. I wait.

It's very cold.

The weapon begins trembling in my hands and I let it drop to the front seat.

I sit on my hands, trying to warm them while the cold breeze blows. Idiot. Do this and how long before you're in jail, and then on trial before a jury of friends or relatives of those fine citizens you gun down tonight?

I start up the truck and let the heater sigh itself on, and then I roll up the window and slowly drive away, lights still off.

"Fool," I say to myself, "remember who you are." And with the truck's lights now on, I drive home. To what's left of it.

DAYS LATER, THERE'S A FRESH smell to the air in my house, for I've done a lot of cleaning and painting, trying not only to bring everything back to where it was but also to spruce up the place. The only real problem has been in the main room, where the words GO HOME were marked in bright red on the white plaster wall. It took me three coats to cover that up, and of course I ended up doing the entire room.

The house is dark and it's late. I'm waiting on the porch with a glass of wine in my hand, watching a light snow fall on Lake Marie. Every light in the house is off and the only illumination comes from the fireplace, which needs more wood.

But I'm content to dawdle. I'm finally at peace after these difficult weeks in Nansen. Finally, I'm beginning to remember who I really am.

I sip my wine, waiting, and then comes the sound of the snowmobiles. I see their wavering dots of light racing across the lake, doing their bit for charity. How wonderful. I raise my glass in salute, the noise of the snowmobiles getting louder as they head across the lake in a straight line.

I put the wineglass down, walk into the living room and toss the last few pieces of wood onto the fire. The sudden heat warms my face in a pleasant glow. The wood isn't firewood, though. It's been shaped and painted by man, and as the flames leap up and devour the lumber, I see the letters begin to fade: DANGER! THIN ICE!

I stroll back to the porch, pick up the wineglass and wait.

Below me, on the peaceful ice of Lake Marie, my new home for my new life, the headlights go by.

And then, one by one, they blink out, and the silence is wonderful.

Anne Perry is one of the most successful historical mystery writers in the world. Her two series, one featuring Inspector Thomas Pitt solving crime in the Victorian era, the other starring 1850s police detective William Monk, have both won acclaim and large audiences. The latest novels in each series are *Pentecost Alley* and *Cain His Brother*, respectively. She makes history come alive again in this story of risk and treachery during the French Revolution.

The Escape
ANNE PERRY

The rescue from the prison of La Force was very carefully planned. Sebastien had taken care of every detail himself, and no one had been told anything they did not have to know. By eight in the evening everyone was in his place.

Jacques was doing no more than driving the coach which had taken them all to La Force, where the man they had come for was lodged pending his trial before the Commander of Public Safety, and inevitably his execution by the guillotine.

He was a young aristocrat named Maximilien de Fleury who was there simply because his father's estates had been confiscated and it was necessary to indict him also in order that they could remain in the hands—and in the pockets—of the government. No other charges were known against him beyond those of idleness and wealth, in Paris in 1792, a crime unto death.

A bribe had been very carefully placed so that his family might visit him for one last time. A plea for clemency, plus several sous, had obtained the promise from a guard to find himself otherwise occupied, so that they might have time alone, during which some swift changes would take place. A very fine forgery executed by Philippe was to be substituted for their pass documents, and in the torchlight four of them would leave where three had come in.

Nicolette was very good indeed at distracting people's concentration by a variety of means, as seemed most suitable according to the nature and status of those whose attention was to be held. She was not a beautiful girl in the usual sense, but she could affect beauty in such a way that it beguiled the mind. One saw the grace and the confidence in her walk, the vitality in her, the imagination and intelligence, and a certain air of courage which intrigued.

She could discard it as quickly and be timid, gentle, demure. Or she could be weary and frightened and appeal for help. She had even aroused the respect of guards Sebastien had thought beyond the human decencies. It never ceased to surprise him, because over the last year he had come to know something of the woman beneath the facade. She had joined the small group in the beginning, two years ago when they had just banded together, tentatively at first, to rescue a friend from one of the many prisons in Paris, before he faced trial and death. There were five of them, Sebastien, Nicolette, Etienne, Philippe the forger, and now Jacques.

Another rescue had followed swiftly, and then a third. By the end of 1792 they had snatched several more people from the Committee's prisons, and failed with three. This year they had attempted more, and succeeded.

Now Sebastien was walking beside Nicolette, her head bent demurely, as they passed the guards and gave them their papers, identifying them as Citizen de Fleury's sister and brother-in-law, come, with the jailor's generous permission, to visit him a last time. A few paces behind them Etienne followed, named in the same document as a brother. All of them, as always, wore a slight disguise, so they would not easily be recognized again. Sometimes it was powdered hair, sometimes a false beard or moustache, a change of complexion with a little paint, a blemish, and of course different clothes.

They walked slowly; it was a natural thing to do in the cold, torchlit passages towards the entrance of the cells. Their feet echoed on the stone floor and the darkness beyond the flame's glare seemed filled with sighs and whispers, as if all the pain of the thousands of inmates was left here after their shivering bodies had been taken out for the last time. Nicolette moved closer to Sebastien, and without thought he put his arm round her.

They presented their identification and their notes of permission to the turnkey and slowly, every movement as if in a dream, he took them, perused them, and passed them back. Then he lifted his great iron keys and placed one in the lock. The bolts fell with a clang, and he pushed open the door.

With a barely perceptible shudder Sebastien went in, his finger to his lips where the guard could not see it, in silent warning. De Fleury looked round, his face white with fear, to see who had intruded on him at this hour. It was only too apparent he expected the worst: a hasty trial and summary execution at first light. It was not uncommon.

"Maximilien!" Nicolette ran to him and threw her arms round him, her lips close to his ear. Sebastien knew she would be telling him not to show surprise or ignorance, that they had come to rescue him and he must follow their lead in everything they said.

Sebastien went after her across the icy, straw-covered floor and wrung de Fleury by the hand, his eyes steady, warning.

The turnkey banged the door shut. Sebastien's heart was in his mouth, his ears straining. The lock did not turn. The man's footsteps died away as he went back up the corridor. Etienne stood guard, shifting nervously from one foot to the other.

"Quickly!" Sebastien took off his cloak, a large mantle of a garment, and held it out to de Fleury. "Put it on," he ordered.

"They'll never let me out!" de Fleury protested, his eyes wild as hope and reason fought in his mind. "Three of you came in, they'll know to let only three of you out. And if you think finding the wrong one will make them let you go, you are dreaming. They'll execute you in my place, simply for aiding my escape. Don't you know that?" Some innate sense of honour forbade him accepting on these terms, but he could not withdraw his hand from the cloak.

"We have passes for four to leave," Sebastien explained. "The turnkey has been bribed to be elsewhere, and it is the changing of the guard who let us in. Be quick."

De Fleury hesitated only a moment. Incredulity turned to wonder in his face, and then relief. He seized the cloak and swung it round his shoulders even as he was moving towards the door.

"Don't run!" Etienne hissed at him.

De Fleury stopped, twisting round to look back at Sebastien.

"You're supposed to be taking your last leave of your family," Sebastien reminded him. "You aren't going to gallop out!"

"Oh . . . oh yes." De Fleury controlled himself with an effort, straightened his shoulders, and walked with agonizingly measured pace out through the cell door and along the torchlit passage towards the entrance. Once he even looked back as if to someone he knew.

Etienne and Nicolette came close behind him, and Sebastien last, closing the cell door, the new pass papers in his hand, for four people.

Nicolette moved ahead to catch up with de Fleury, clasping his arm and clinging to it. Every attitude of her body expressed grief.

They were twenty feet short of the outer gates. The guards moved across the passage to block their way. Sebastien felt his heart beating so hard his body shook with the violence of it. It was difficult to get his breath.

De Fleury faltered. Was Nicolette leaning on him, or in fact supporting him?

One of the guards brandished a musket.

De Fleury stopped. Etienne and Sebastien drew level with him and stopped also.

"Here," Sebastien offered the pass to the guard. He took it and read it, looking carefully from one to the other of them. Their faces were full of shadows in the torchlight. Each one stood motionless, at once afraid to meet their eyes, and afraid not to.

This was the relief guard. They had not seen them come in. The paper was for the exact number of people, three men and one woman.

There was no sound but the guard's breath rasping in his throat and the hiss and flicker of the torches in their brackets.

"Right," the guard said at last. "Out." He gestured to the great archway and on shaking legs de Fleury went down, Nicolette still at his side. It had begun to rain.

Sebastien and Etienne increased their pace, passing into the wide street. Etienne took Nicolette by the arm almost exactly as the shot rang out in the air above them.

They froze.

One of the guards came running through the archway and across the cobbles, his musket held in both hands, ready to raise and fire.

Sebastien swivelled round. He was about to ask what was the matter, when he saw the turnkey behind them, and the ugly truth leaped to his mind only too clearly.

"Citizen de Fleury!" the guard accused breathlessly, looking from one to the other of them.

Before de Fleury could move, Etienne put his hand on his arm and stepped forward himself.

"What is it? Is something wrong?"

The guard stared at him, trying to discern his features in the erratic light.

Sebastien peered to see how far away the carriage was. Would Jacques have the cool-headedness to bring it forward even after he heard the musket shot? If not, they were lost.

The turnkey was coming out into the street as well, torch in his hand.

"Is it not bad enough we have to lose our brother, without bothering us at this time?" Etienne demanded, his voice shaking.

Sebastien heard the carriage wheels on the cobbles and saw the faint light on Jacques' pale hair. He turned back and caught Nicolette's eyes. He nodded imperceptibly.

Nicolette began to sink as if she would faint.

Sebastien started forward and picked her up, swinging past the guard and knocking the musket sideways and onto the stones. Etienne grasped de Fleury by the arm and as the carriage drew level, threw the door open, and pushed him in with all his might. De Fleury fell onto the floor, with Nicolette on top of him.

There were shouts of fury from the archway and swaying light as the turnkey came up, yelling for them to stop.

Sebastien knocked the barrel of the gun into the air, and then hauled himself onto the footplate at the side of the carriage just as it turned and picked up speed, and a moment later a musket shot rang out, and another, and another. One thudded into the woodwork, but it was nearly a yard away. Please God, Etienne was on the footplate.

They would call out the National Guard, of course they would, but by then de Fleury would be on the road to Calais, and they would be back in the familiar streets and alleys of the Cordeliers district, invisible again—if only they could elude them for the next hour.

The rain was heavier, driving in his face, making a mist of the dark streets, dampening torches, sliming the cobbles under the horses' feet. The wood under Sebastien's fingers was wet as he clung on while the coach swayed and lurched along the Rue Saint Antoine towards the Place de la Bastille. He could still hear the sound of gunfire behind.

Was Etienne on the footplate, clinging on as he was, or had he been flung off, and was lying somewhere on the road, perhaps injured, or even dead. Perhaps one of the shots had caught him?

Jacques could see better in the dark than he could! They were close to the river. He could smell the water and see the faint gleam of reflections on the surface. They must be on the Quai de l'Hôtel de Ville. There were still shouts behind them, and another volley of shots. They were far too exposed in the open.

They swerved left into the Pont d'Arcole. The huge mass of Notre Dame loomed ahead on the Île de la Cité. They must find the narrow streets soon, the winding alleys of their own district.

They swept through an open square, more shots splattering around them, some sharp on the stones, others thudding heavily into the woodwork of the carriage. The driving rain was making it desperately hard to cling on. Sebastien was slithering wildly, his fingers bruised, his body aching. All his muscles seemed locked.

He was all but thrown off as they careered over the Petit Pont, across the Quai Saint-Michel, and finally into the narrow streets behind the Church of Saint Severin.

When at last they stopped in the stable yard in the flaring torchlight, Sebastien was so numb he could barely let go. His fingers would not unbend. He saw Philippe's face white and streaked with rain as he ran out of the shelter of the doorway. The horses were shivering and streaked dark with sweat.

Sebastien dropped down onto the cobbles and almost fell, his body was so stiff, and hurt as if he had been battered.

"What happened?" Philippe demanded. "You look awful!" He looked at the coach, and his voice dropped. "It's riddled with splinters—a shot!"

He lunged forward and yanked the door open, and Nicolette almost fell out. She was ashen.

Jacques scrambled off the box and came round the side. He too was soaked with rain, his hat was gone, and he looked exhausted and terrified. His eyes went straight to Sebastien.

"Etienne?" Sebastien asked the question which was in all their minds. "Where's Etienne? And de Fleury? Is he all right?"

Nicolette stared at him and shook her head minutely, barely a movement at all. "De Fleury's dead," she said in a small, tired voice. "One of the musket balls must have caught him. I don't even know when it happened. In the dark I didn't see, and he didn't cry out. In fact I never heard him speak at all. It could—it could have been the very first moment, when they were shooting at us before we even left the prison yard, or any time until we left them behind when we crossed the river."

There was a clatter of boots on the stones, and Etienne came round the back of the coach. He looked pale and very wet. There was blood on the sleeve of his coat, but he seemed otherwise unharmed.

Sebastien felt a surge of relief, and then instant guilt. He took the torch from Philippe and went to the coach, the door still swinging open as Nicolette had left it, and peered in.

De Fleury was half lying on the seat, the cape Sebastien had put round him in the prison crumpled, covering his body, his legs buckled as if he had been thrown violently when the coach had lurched from side to side as the horses careered through the darkness, shots screaming past them, thudding into the wood and ricocheting from the walls of the buildings on either side.

Sebastien held the torch higher so he could see de Fleury's face. With his other hand he moved the cloak aside. There was no mistaking death. The wide-open, sightless eyes were already glazed. He looked oddly surprised, as if in spite of all the terror of the prison, and then the sudden escape, the flight and the shooting of the guards behind him, he had not expected it.

Nicolette was close behind him. He handed her the torch and she held it, shaking a little, the light wavering, so he could use both hands to move de Fleury.

"What are we going to do with him?" she asked over his shoulder.

He had not yet thought as far as that. Other failures had stopped far earlier, before they had ever reached the prisoners, or else very soon after. Once before they had fled in rout, but the prisoner had remained behind, to face the guillotine. Decent disposal of the corpse had not been their responsibility. There were no churches open since the edict, and no priests in Paris openly. Religion was outlawed. You could go to the guillotine simply for harbouring a priest, let alone indulging in the rites of the faith.

Yet they could not simply leave him. They had offered him freedom, and now he was dead.

"I'll smuggle him outside Paris, as we were going to." It was Etienne's voice from the yard, behind Nicolette, his face wet in the torchlight, but he was beginning to regain his composure. "I'll bury him somewhere on the road to Calais." He grimaced. "At least that's better than a common grave with the other victims of the day's execution. Better a quiet coach ride towards Calais than a drive through the street mobs in a tumbrel."

"Yes, you'd better do that," Sebastien agreed. "Thank you." He leaned forward to straighten the cloak, to lift it and cover the face. In spite of the thousands who had died in the city since the storming of the Bastille nearly three years ago, the small gestures of decency still mattered—or perhaps because of them.

Etienne mistook his intention.

"Leave him there," he said quickly. "I'll take him out before dawn. Better in the dark. I'll make it look as if he's sleeping."

"Good," Sebastien acknowledged. "Thank you." He looked a moment longer at de Fleury's dead face. He felt guilty. Perhaps this death was better than the guillotine with all its deliberate horror, but that was little comfort now. They had still let him down. How had it happened? As always, no one else had known anything of their plans. They had been made only the night before. Why had the guard come back, and then followed them out to challenge them?

"I'm sorry," he whispered to de Fleury. He should leave him sitting up a little better. There was no point. It was a meaningless thing to do, but he still did it. It lent a kind of dignity.

Then he saw the hole in the back of the seat where the musket ball had come through. What an irony that the one ball that had penetrated through instead of merely splintering the wood and lodging in the upholstery, should have gone straight to his heart. There was blood on the seat, dark and shiny. Sebastien put his finger to the neat round hole, then froze. He had touched the ball, embedded in the wadding. That was impossible!

His mind whirled, bombarded with realisations that ended in one terrible, irreversible fact. De Fleury had been shot from the front, from inside the coach! That could only be either Nicolette or Etienne—or just conceivably Jacques, if he had somehow tied the reins for a few moments and swung down from the box, and in the confusion and the dark Nicolette had not seen him.

But why? Why on earth would any of them, people he had trusted with his life over and over again, kill de Fleury?

Nicolette was standing at his elbow, still holding the torch. Etienne was still waiting.

"Yes," Sebastien said steadily, moving back and away from the carriage door. He slammed it shut, turning to face them. Nicolette lowered the torch. It must be getting heavy. "Yes, that's a good idea." He did not know what else to say. The question roared round in his head: which one of them—and why?

He did not want to know. The friendships were too deep and too precious. The betrayal was hideous. But he had to know. The suspicion would stain them all, and worse than that, they could no longer trust any life to whoever had done this. It explained the guard's return, the shots, everything else.

It was still raining. They were all standing there watching him. Nicolette, her hair wet across her brow, her clothes sticking to her, her dress sodden; Etienne with his arm still bleeding, holding it across his chest now, to ease the weight of it; Jacques frightened and puzzled; Philippe beginning, as usual, to get cross. He had been waiting for them since they left, not knowing what had happened.

Sebastien forced himself to smile. "Let's go inside and at least have something hot to drink. I don't know about the rest of you, but I'm frozen!"

There was a sigh of relief, a release of long-held tension. As one, they turned and followed him towards the light and the warmth.

Sebastien slept from sheer exhaustion, but when he woke in the morning, late and with his head pounding, the question returned almost instantly. One of them had killed de Fleury, coldly and deliberately. When the rescue had succeeded, in spite of the betrayal of the plan to the guards, they had shot him in the coach as they fled through the night.

How? None of them had taken a gun into the prison. It would have been suicidal. It must have been left in the coach, against the eventuality of the escape not being foiled by the guards. That still meant that any of the three of them could have done it, Jacques most easily, he had obtained the coach, that had been his task. But it would have been very hard for him to have left the box and come into the coach to perform the act. When they were in a straight road, Nicolette would have been likely to have seen him.

Nicolette would have found it the easiest. It was she who had ridden in the coach alone with de Fleury. When had she put the gun there? He sat at the table in his rooms eating a breakfast of hot chocolate and two slices of bread. It was stale, but bread was scarce these days, and expensive. He went over the events of the previous day, from the time Jacques had brought the coach until they had left from the prison of La Force.

There was no time when Nicolette had been alone. She had helped Philippe with the forged papers, getting them exactly right, then she had been with Sebastien himself.

The question that remained was why? Why would Etienne have wished de Fleury dead? How did he even know him? If he had some bitter enmity with him, why had he not simply said so, and refused to be part of the rescue?

There was no alternative but to confront him with the evidence and demand the truth, at the same time hoping against reason that there was some explanation that did not damn him.

IT WAS EARLY EVENING WHEN Sebastien knocked on the door of Etienne's rooms in the Rue de Seine. He had put it off all day, but it could wait no longer.

The door swung open and Etienne stood in the entrance, smiling.

"Sebastien!" he said with surprise and apparent pleasure. "Not another rescue? It must be someone very important for you to try now, so soon after this fiasco."

"No, not another escape. An answer, if you have one."

Etienne's fair eyebrows shot up. "To what?"

"To why you betrayed us to the guard, and when that didn't work, why you shot de Fleury?"

Etienne stood motionless, his eyes unblinking. Seconds ticked by before he spoke. He measured Sebastien's nerve, weighed their friendship and all that they had shared, the dangers, the exultation of success and the bitterness of failures, and knew denial was no use.

"How did you know?" he said finally.

"The ball was still in the hole behind him. He was shot from in front."

"Careless of me," Etienne said with a very slight shrug. "I didn't see it. Thought it would be so far embedded in the wadding you'd never find it."

"I wouldn't have, if I hadn't put my finger in."

Etienne still had not moved. "Why not Nicolette? She was in there with him."

"You left the gun in the carriage . . . in case. She had no chance to do that."

"I see."

"Why?" Sebastien asked. "What was de Fleury to you?"

Etienne moved backward into the room, an elegant room with mementos of a more precious age, when it was still acceptable to be an aristocrat and have a coat of arms. One hung on the farther wall, two crossed swords beneath it.

"Nothing," Etienne replied. "Or to you either . . . compared with our friendship." He was not begging, there was something almost like amusement in his eyes, and regret, but no fear.

Then suddenly he darted backward with startling speed. His arm swung up and he grasped one of the swords from the wall and in an instant was

facing Sebastien with it held low and pointing at him, ready to lunge. There
was sadness in his eyes, but no wavering at all. He meant death, and he
had both the will and the art to accomplish it.

They faced each other for a fraction of time so small it was barely
measurable, then Sebastien threw himself to one side and scrambled to his
feet as Etienne lunged forward. The blade ripped the chair open where a
second before he had been standing.

There was no weapon for Sebastien. The other sword was still on the
wall, ten feet away and behind Etienne. There was a silver candlestick on
the table near the wall to his left. He dived towards it and his hand closed
over it as Etienne darted forward again. The blade flickered like a shaft of
light, drawing a thin thread of blood from Sebastien's arm and sending a
sheet of pain through his flesh.

He parried Etienne's attack with the candlestick, but it was a poor defense, and he knew from Etienne's face that it would last only moments.
The sword was twelve inches longer, lighter and faster.

His only chance was to throw the candlestick. Yet once it was out of his
hands he had nothing left. He must work his way round until he could
snatch the other sword. But if that was obvious to him, then it would be
to Etienne also.

He picked up a light chair with his other hand, and threw it. It barely
interrupted Etienne's balance, but it did bring Sebastien a yard nearer to
the wall and the sword.

"You're wasting your time, Sebastien," Etienne said quietly, but for all
the lightness of his voice, there was pain in it. He would not have had it
come to this, but when he had to choose between himself and another, then
it would always be himself. "I'm a better swordsman than you'll ever be.
I'm an aristocrat, for whatever that's worth. I was born to the saddle and
the sword. Don't fight me, and I'll make it quick . . . clean."

Sebastien picked up a Sevres vase and threw it at him.

"Damn! You shouldn't have broken that, you bloody barbarian!"
Etienne said with disgust. He slashed and caught Sebastien a glancing blow
across the other arm, ripping his shirt and drawing another thin line of
beaded blood.

Sebastien jumped over the footstool and dived for the other sword.
Etienne saw what he was aiming for and leaped after him, but his foot
caught the stool and he crashed down, saving himself by putting out his
other hand. Had he not fallen, he would have speared Sebastien through
the chest.

Sebastien tore the weapon off its mounting and faced him just as he rose
to his feet again. The blades clashed, crossed, withdrew, and clashed again.
They swayed back and forth, dodging the furniture, first one slipping, then

the other. Sebastien was stronger and he had the longer reach, but Etienne had by far the greater skill. It could only be a matter of time until he saw the fatal advantage, and Sebastien knew it.

There had been far too much death already. Paris was reeking with death and the fear of death. There was so much that was good in Etienne, far more than in many that were still alive. He had courage, gaiety, imagination, the gift for inspiring others to give of their best, to rise above what they had thought they were and find new heights.

Then Sebastien again saw in his mind's eye the surge of hope in de Fleury's face when he knew why they had come to La Force, the gratitude, and then the surprise of death as he knew he was betrayed.

He stepped back and with all his strength tore one of the tapestries off the wall and threw it at Etienne. Etienne swore, as much for the damage of the fabric as anything else. He ducked so that it did not entangle him, and at the same moment Sebastien lunged forward and sideways and his blade sank deep into flesh. Etienne fell, taking the sword with him, blood staining his shirt in a dark tide.

Sebastien stood still, looking down at him. There was surprise in his victory, and no pleasure at all, not even any satisfaction. Etienne was dead with the single thrust.

Sebastien pulled out the blade and let it fall towards the body. He felt empty except for an overwhelming sadness, a heaviness inside him as if he could hardly carry his own weight.

As he had with de Fleury the night before, he bent to the body, only this was different, this was a man who had been his friend, a man he himself had killed. He wanted to say something, but all that filled his mind was "Why?" Why would a man like Etienne have shot de Fleury? Why could he not have told Sebastien, if de Fleury were some bitter enemy from the past?

Then he saw the paper in Etienne's pocket, just a small edge poking out. He pulled it, then opened it up. It was a large sheet of high-quality vellum, written in a copperplate hand. It appeared to be a legal document, but quite short, taking up only two thirds of the page. After it were several signatures.

He began to read:

Versailles, 5th June, 1785.

I, Maximilien Honoré de Fleury, Vicomte de Lauzun, do herewith offer myself and all I have in solemn covenant with Satan, Lord of Darkness and of Lies, Master of Destruction, King of the Nether World, and Heir Apparent of this Earth and all that is in it, that I may be of service to him, in the seduction of innocence, the indulgence of appetite, the sacrifice of human flesh to his will, and the bending of minds to his dominion. For my loyalty to his cause he will reward me with pleasure and riches here, endless sensation and variety, and hereafter a place among the Lords of his Kingdom.

I pledge my soul to this cause, and write my name in my own blood . . . Maximilien Honoré de Fleury.

In witness to this covenant we fellow servants of his Satanic Majesty do sign our names beneath:

Jean Sylvain Marie Dessalines
Jean Marie Victor Coritot
Stanislas Marie Delabarre
Donatien Royou
Joseph Augustin Barère
Etienne Jacques Marie du Bac
Ignace Georges Legendre

He stared at the page, unable to believe it. Etienne had been witness to this grotesque piece of . . . of what? Did these men really believe they had made a pact with the devil? Perhaps in 1785 it had seemed some kind of effete joke. Now no one joked about the devil, he was only too real. The stench of his breath was everywhere and the mark of his hand shrivelled the heart.

People had turned on each other, killing and being killed. That Etienne, of all people, ironic, graceful, and brave, should have taken de Fleury's life to protect this grubby secret was tragic above all. If he had told Sebastien about it, Sebastien would have taken the paper from de Fleury, and made him promise on his life to keep silence. He could hardly tell his hosts in England of Etienne's complicity without exposing his own, and destroying his welcome also.

Sebastien shivered, cold through to his bones. Perhaps that was how pacts with the devil worked—you lost sight of the stupidity of evil, and the ultimate sanity of good. You destroyed yourself—unnecessarily.

He put the letter in his pocket. He would burn it when he got home. He turned round and went out of the door and closed it softly behind him.

Ruth Rendell is also no stranger to these pages. Her stories of psychological suspense always reveal a new twist in the human psyche that seemed to be just waiting for an author like her to reveal it. The author of over twenty novels and innumerable short stories, she explores the dark recesses of the mind that make men and women like the successful career woman in "Clothes" do unexplainable things.

Clothes
RUTH RENDELL

"I'd like this, please."

She had put the dress down on the counter. The look the assistant gave her was slightly apprehensive. Alison had sounded breathless, she had sounded elated. Now that it was too late she restrained herself.

"How would you like to pay?"

Instead of answering, she laid the credit card on the counter where the dress was now being folded, amid layers of tissue paper. The bill came waving out of the machine and she signed in the too-small space on the right-hand side. At this point, and it was always the same, she couldn't wait to get away. Lingering, chatting to the assistant—"You'll get a lot of wear out of this one," "Enjoy wearing it"—embarrassed her. She felt as if she was there on false pretences or as if her secret self must inevitably be revealed. She walked off quickly and she was happy, she felt the familiar buzz, the swing of light-headedness, the rush of adrenaline. She had made her day, she had bought something.

Once outside, she took the dress out of the bag and put it into her briefcase along with the outline plans for the Grimwood project. That way the people in the office would not know what she had been doing. The carrier went into a litter bin and the bill with it. A taxi came and she got into it. Already the level of excitement had begun to flag. By the time she walked into the PR consultancy of which she was chief executive none of it was left. She smiled and told her assistant lunch had gone on longer than expected.

On the way home she bought something else. She didn't mean to. But that went without saying, for she scarcely ever did mean to. It was where she lived, she sometimes thought, the dangerous place she lived in, Knightsbridge, shopping country. If she and Gil moved out into the sticks, some distant suburb . . . She knew they wouldn't.

She should have had a taxi to her doorstep, not used the tube. Some of it was the fault of the dress, for now she knew she disliked the dress—the colour, the cut. She would never wear it, and the amount she had spent on it printed itself on her mind in black letters. The elation it had brought her had turned to panic. Absurdly, she had taken the tube to save money, because it cost ninety pence and a taxi would have been five pounds. But it gave her a half-mile walk down Sloane Street. At six, on late-closing night.

Sometimes Alison thought of the things she might have done at leisure in London. Gone to the National Gallery, the Wallace Collection, walked in the parks, joined the London Library. She had heard the Museum of the Moving Image was wonderful. Instead she went shopping. She bought things. Well, she bought clothes. Halfway down the long street of shops, her eye was caught by a sweater in a window. The feeling was familiar, the faint breathlessness, the drying mouth, the words repeated in her head—she must have it, she must have it. On these occasions she seemed to see the future so clearly. She seemed to live in advance the regret she would feel if she didn't have the thing, whatever it was. The remorse experienced when she *did* have it was forgotten.

The knob on the shop door was a heavy glass ball, set in brass. She closed her hand over the knob. She paused. But that was not unusual. Hesitating on the doorstep, she told herself she was buying this sweater because she had made a mistake with the dress. She didn't like the dress, but the sweater would make up for that. She turned the knob and the door came open. Inside, a woman sat at a gilded table with a marble top. She lifted her head, smiled at Alison, and said, "Hi." Alison knew the woman wouldn't get up and come over and start showing her things, it wasn't that kind of shop, and Alison knew about shops. She went to the rail where the sweater and its fellows hung. The fever was already upon her and reason gone. This feeling was like a combination of sexual excitement and the effect of a strong drink. When it had her in its clutch she stopped thinking, or rather, she thought only of the garment before her; how it would look on her, where she would wear it and when, how possessing it would change her life for the better.

Shopping had to be done in a rush. That was part of the whole character of it. Do it fast and do it impulsively. The blood beat in her head. She took the sweater off its hanger, held it up against herself.

The woman said, "Would you like to try it on?"

"I'll have it," Alison said. She took an identical sweater off the rail, but in a darker shade. "In fact, I'll have both." She responded to the assistant's smile with a radiant smile of her own.

When she had paid and was outside the shop once more, she looked at her watch and saw that the whole transaction had taken seven minutes. The two sweaters were too bulky to go in the briefcase, so she took out the dress and put it in the black shiny white-lettered bag with her new purchases. She began to think of how she was going to get into the flat without Gil seeing she had been shopping.

He might not yet be home. Sometimes he came in first, sometimes she did. If he was home, she might be able to get into the bedroom and hide the bag before he saw. If the worst came to the worst and he saw the bag, he would suppose there was only one garment inside it, not three. The buzz was easing up, the adrenaline was being absorbed, and she understood something else: that this was the first time she had bought something without trying it on first.

The glass doors opened for her and she walked in. She went up in the lift. Her key slipped into the lock and turned and the front door opened. It was impossible to tell if he was there or not. She called out, "Gil?" and his voice answering from the kitchen, "I'm in here," made her jump. She ran into the bedroom and thrust the bag into the back of the clothes cupboard. It was his evening to cook. She had forgotten. When she was shopping she forgot everything else. She went into the kitchen and put her arms around him and kissed him. He was wearing an apron and holding a wooden spoon.

"Tell me," he said. "Do you actually like dried tomatoes?"

"Dried tomatoes? I've never thought about it. Well, no, I don't suppose I do, really."

"No one does. That's my great culinary discovery of the week. No one does but they pretend to, like they do about green peppers."

He enlarged on this. Gil produced a cookery programme for television and he began telling her about a soufflé that kept going wrong. At the fourth attempt, the star of the programme, a temperamental man, had picked up and upended the spoiled soufflé over the head of one of the camera crew. Alison listened and laughed in the right places and told him about the latest developments in the Grimwood account. He said he'd give her a shout when the food was ready and she went away into the bedroom to change.

Every evening, if they weren't going out, she changed into jeans or track-suit pants and a sweatshirt. The irony was that these were old, she had had them for years, while the cupboard groaned under the weight of new clothes. There was barely room for the new dress and the sweaters to squeeze in. When would she wear any of them? Perhaps never. Perhaps, unworn, they would join the stack that must soon be packed into her largest suitcase and taken to the hospice shop.

They loved her in the hospice shop. They called her Alison, they knew her so well. "What lovely clothes you always bring us, Alison," and, "You have quite a turnover in clothes, Alison—well, you must have in your job." They could probably run the hospice for a week on what they raised by the sale of her clothes.

It was an addiction, it was like alcoholism or drugs or gambling, and more expensive than drinking or the fruit machines. Last week, when she was coming in with a bright yellow bag and an olive-green bag, Gil had caught her in the hall. Caught her. She had used the words inadvertently, without thinking, and inaccurately. For Gil was the kindest and best of men, he would never, never reproach her. The worst thing was that he would *praise* her. He would tell her it was her money, she earned more than he did anyway, she could do what she liked with it. Why shouldn't she buy herself some new clothes?

She had imagined telling him then, when they came face-to-face and she had those bags in her hands. She imagined confessing, saying, I've something to tell you. His face would change, he would think what everyone thought when they heard those words from their partner. She would sit on the floor at his feet—all this she imagined, building an absurd scenario—and hold his hand and tell him, I do this, I am mad, it's driving me mad, and I can't stop. I keep buying clothes. Not jewelry or ornaments or furniture or pictures, not stuff to put on my face or my hair, not even shoes or hats or gloves. I buy clothes. A dress shop is a wine bar to me. It is my casino. I can't pass it. If I go into a department store to buy a box of tissues or a bathmat, I go upstairs, I buy clothes.

He would laugh. He would be happy and relieved because she was telling him she liked buying things to wear, not that she'd met someone else and was leaving him. Kisses then and reassurances and a heartening, Why shouldn't you spend your own money? He, who was so understanding, wouldn't understand this.

His voice called out, "Alison! It's ready."

They were to have a glass of wine first. This wine had been much praised on the programme and he wanted her to try it. He raised his glass to her. "Do you know what today is?"

Some anniversary. It was women who were supposed to remember these things, not men. "Should I? Oh, dear."

"Not the first time we met," he said. "Not even the first time you took me out to dinner. The first time *I* took *you* out. Three years ago today."

She put into the words all the emotion with which her thoughts had charged her. "I love you."

Gil scarcely knew what clothes she possessed. He never looked in her cupboard. Sometimes, when she wore one of the new dresses or suits or shirts, he would say, "I like that. It's new, isn't it?"

"I've had it for ages. You must have seen it before."

And he accepted that. He didn't notice clothes much, he wasn't interested. But when he asked, she should have told him. Or when the credit-card statements came in. Instead of paying the huge sums secretly, she should have said, "Look at this. This is what I do with my money. This is my madness and you must stop me."

She couldn't. She was too ashamed. She even wondered what the credit-card people must think of her when month after month they assessed her expenditure and found another thousand pounds gone on clothes. The shop assistants wrote "clothes" in the space on the chit and she had once thought, stupidly, of asking them to put "goods" instead. It was because of what she was that the humiliation was so intense, because she was clever and accomplished, with a good degree and a dazzling CV, at the top of her profession, sought-after, able to ask fees that raised eyebrows but seldom deterred. And her addiction was the kind that afflicted the football pools winners or sixteen-year-old school-leavers.

They were better than she. At least they were honest and open about it. Some could be frank and admit it, even make a joke of it. A few months back she had travelled to Edinburgh with a client to make a product presentation. They had stayed overnight. Edinburgh is not a place that immediately comes to mind as a shopping centre, while there are many other interesting things to do there, but the client announced as soon as they got into the station taxi that she would like to spend the two hours they had to spare at the shops.

"I'm a compulsive shopper, you know. It's what gives me a buzz."

Alison had said restrainedly, "What did you want to buy?"

"Buy? Oh, I don't know. I know it when I see it."

So Alison had gone shopping with her and seen all the signs and symptoms that she saw in herself, but with one exception. This woman was not ashamed, she was not deceitful.

"I'm crazy, really," she said when she had bought a suit she confessed she "didn't like all that much." "I've got wardrobes full of stuff I never wear." And she laughed merrily. "I suppose you plan everything you buy terribly carefully, don't you?"

And Alison, who had stood by while the suit was bought, sick with desire to buy herself, controlling herself with all her might, wearing what she now feared had been a supercilious half-smile, agreed that this was so. She smiled like a superior being, one who bought clothes when the old ones wore out.

On that trip she had managed to avoid buying anything. The energy expended in denial had left her exhausted. In London, afterwards, she went on a dreadful splurge, like the bulimic's binge. It was that day, or the day after, she had read the piece in the paper about compulsive behaviour. Eating disorders, for instance, indicated some deep-seated emotional disturbance. It was the same with gambling, even with shopping. The compulsive shopper buys as a way of masking a need for love and to cover up inadequacy.

It wasn't true. She loved Gil. She had everything she wanted. Her life was good and satisfying. The compulsion to buy had only begun when she realised she was rich, she had more than enough, she could afford it now. Only she couldn't, hardly anyone could. Hardly anyone's income could stand this drain on it.

Compulsive shopping was a cry for help. That was what the psychologists said. But help for what? For help to stop compulsive shopping?

PASSING THE SHOP WHERE SHE had bought the sweaters—in a taxi, for safety's sake—she reflected on something she had thought of only momentarily at the time. She had bought the sweaters without trying them on. It was as if she was saying, I don't care if they fit or not, that is not why I am buying them, I want to *buy*, not to have.

The office was in the city, in a part where there were few shops. This, of course, was a blessing, yet she had recognised lately her dissatisfaction with the absence of clothes shops, the peculiar kind of *hunger* this lack brought her. Once she was outside in the street, an almost overwhelming impulse came to get in a taxi and be taken to where the shops were. She managed to resist. She had work to do, she had to be at her desk, near those phones, beside that fax machine. But as the days passed, the shopless days, she began to think, It will be all right for me to go shopping next time I have the opportunity, it won't be sick, it won't be neurotic, because it has been so long, it has been a whole week. . . .

There was an evening when it rained and she couldn't find a taxi. Again she took the tube and at Knightsbridge looked for a taxi to take her that half mile. It was quite possible to walk home by residential streets, there were many options, and it was one of the most charming parts of London. Even in the rain. But compulsive shopping began before she came to the shops, she had learnt that now, it was what led her steps to Sloane Street when she might so easily have taken Seville Street and Lowndes Square.

Her thoughts were strange. She recognised them as strange. Mad, perhaps. She was thinking that if she controlled herself this evening, she would not have to do so on the following day. Next day, after the client conference, she would find herself in Piccadilly, at the bottom of Bond Street, and if she walked up towards the tube station, her route would take her along Brook Street and into South Molton Street, into one of the meccas of shopping, into heaven, buying country, shopland.

She passed the shop with the globular glass doorknob and as she came to the next, already able to see ahead of her the gleam of a single shimmering garment isolated in its window, footsteps came running behind her and Gil's arm was around her, his umbrella held high over her head.

"You ought to buy that," he said. "You'd look good in that."

She shuddered. He felt the shudder and looked at her in concern.

"A designer walked over my grave," she said.

It was the time to say she wouldn't buy the dress and tell him why not. She couldn't do it. All she felt was resentment that he had caught up with her and, by his presence and his kind, innocent suggestion, stopped her buying it. He was like the well-intentioned friend who offers the secret drinker a double scotch.

In the morning she went in late, walking up Sloane Street. There was nothing to do before the conference. She went into the shop and bought the dress Gil had said would look good on her. She didn't try it on, but told the surprised assistant it was her size, she knew it would fit. High on adrenaline, she told herself this purchase need not stop her buying later in the day. The day was gone anyway, she thought, it was spoiled by buying the dress and there was no point in taking a stand today, a preliminary shot of the drug had gone in. If control was possible, it could start tomorrow. In the office she took the dress out of her briefcase and stuffed it in a desk drawer.

The conference was over by three. For the past hour or more she had scarcely been attending. Once her own talk was over she lost interest and let her thoughts run in the direction they always did these days. Even during the talk she once or twice lost the thread of what she was saying, needed to refer to her notes, seemed to fumble with words. The company chairman asked her if she was feeling unwell. Sitting down again, taking a drink of water, she looked ahead of her to the great thoroughfare of shops waiting for her, full of things waiting to be bought, sitting there and waiting, and a huge longing took hold of her. She almost ran out of the building, she was breathless and she was thirsty, as if she had never taken a drink of water.

On her way up Bond Street she bought a suit and a jacket. She tried both on, but it was only for form's sake and because she cringed under the shop assistant's surprised look.

A taxi came as if to rescue her while she walked onwards and upwards, carrying her bags, but she let it pass by and turned into Brook Street. By this time, at this *stage* of her indulgence, her feet seemed to lose contact with the ground. She floated or skimmed the surface of the pavement. In the road she was always in danger of being run over. If she had met someone she knew, she would have passed him by unseeing. Her body had undergone chemical changes which had a profound effect on recognition, on logical thought, on rational behaviour. They negated reason. She was unable to control the urge to buy because for these moments, this hour perhaps, she rejected a "cure," she wanted her compulsion, she loved it, she was drunk on it.

Thoughts she had, words in her head, but they were always simple and direct. Why shouldn't I have these things? I can afford them. Why shouldn't I be well-dressed? I mustn't be guilty about this simple enjoyable *happy* pastime. . . . They repeated themselves in her mind as she floated along, aware too of her steadily beating heart.

In South Molton Street she bought a shirt, and in the shop next door a skirt with a sweater that matched it. She tried neither on, and when she was outside something made her look at the label on the skirt and sweater, which showed her she had bought them two sizes too big. She stood there, in the walking street, feeling elation drop, knowing she couldn't go back in there.

She was ashamed. The fall was very swift from reckless excitement to a kind of visionary horror, it slid off her like oversize clothes slipping from her shoulders to the floor, and there came a sudden flash of appalled insight. She began to walk mechanically. Nearly at Oxford Street, she put the new clothes bags into the first rubbish bin she came to. Then she put the suit and the jacket in too. She turned her back and ran.

In the taxi she was crying. The taxi driver said, "Are you okay, love?" She said she wasn't well, she would be all right in a minute. The waste, the wickedness of such waste, were what she thought of. There were thousands, millions, who never had new clothes, who wore hand-downs or rags or just managed to buy secondhand. She had thrown away new clothes.

For some reason she thought of Gil, who trusted and loved her. She couldn't face him again, she would have to go to some hotel for the night. By a tortuous route the taxi was winding through streets behind Broadcasting House, behind Langham Place. It came down into Regent Street and she told the driver to let her off. He didn't like that, and she gave him a five-pound note. What was five pounds? She had just thrown away two hundred times that.

Carrying only her briefcase, she went into a department store. She caught sight of herself in a mirror, her wild hair, her staring eyes, the whiteness of her face: a madwoman. Something else struck her, as she paused there briefly. She wasn't well-dressed, almost any woman she passed was better dressed than she was. Every week, nearly every day, she bought clothes, mountains of clothes, cupboards-full, clothes to be unloaded on charities or thrown away unworn, but she was dressed less well than a woman who bought what she wore out of the money a husband gave her for housekeeping.

She hated clothes. Understanding came in migraine-like flashes of light and darkness. Why had she never realised how she hated clothes? They made her feel sick, the new, slightly bitter smell of them, their sinuous slithering pressures on her, surrounding her as they now did, rails of coats and jackets, suits and dresses. She was in designer country and she could smell and feel, but she saw very little. Her eyes were affected by her mental state, and a mist hung in front of them.

Fumbling, she began to slide clothes off the rail, a shirt here, a sweater there. She opened her briefcase and stuffed the things inside. A label hung out and part of a sleeve when she closed the case. She snatched a knitted garment, long and sleeveless and buttoned, and a blouse of stiff organza, another sweater, another shirt. No one saw her, or if they did, made no attempt to intervene.

She pulled a scarf from a shelf and wound it round her neck. Pulling at the ends, she thought how good it would be to lose consciousness, for the scarf quietly to strangle her. With her overflowing briefcase, too full to close, she began to walk down the stairs. No one came after her. No one had seen. On her way through leather goods she picked up a handbag, though it was unusual for her to be attracted by such things, then a wallet and a pair of gloves. She held them in one hand, while the other held the briefcase, the bigger garments over her arm.

Between the inner glass doors and the entrance doors a bell began ringing urgently. The security officer approached. She sat down on the floor with all the stolen things around her and when he came up to her, she said quite sanely, though with a break in her voice, "Help me, someone help me."

A winner of the Anthony Award and the Lifetime Achievement Award from the Private Eye Writers of America, Marcia Muller also writes gritty, detailed westerns as well as excellent mystery stories. But her female detective Sharon McCone, whose caseload was collected last year in *The McCone Files*, does not even make an appearance here. Instead, "The Cracks in the Sidewalk" focuses on the lives of two very different women, and what happens when their paths cross.

The Cracks in the Sidewalk
MARCIA MULLER

Gracie

I'm leaning against my mailbox and the sun's shining on my face and my pigeons are coming round. Storage box number 27368. The mail carrier's already been here—new one, because he didn't know my name and kind of shied away from me like I smell bad. Which I probably do. I'll have him trained soon, though, and he'll say "Hi, Gracie" and pass the time of day and maybe bring me something to eat. Just the way the merchants in this block do. It's been four years now, and I've got them all trained. Box 27368—it's gotten to be like home.

Home . . .

Nope, I can't think about that. Not anymore.

Funny how the neighborhood's changed since I started taking up space on this corner with my cart and my pigeons, on my blanket on good days, on plastic in the rain. Used to be the folks who lived in this part of San Francisco was Mexicans and the Irish ran the bars and used-furniture stores. Now you see a lot of Chinese or whatever, and there're all these new restaurants and coffeehouses. Pretty fancy stuff. But that's okay; they draw a nice class of people, and the waiters bring me the leftovers. And my pigeons are still the same—good company. They're sort of like family.

Family . . .

No, I can't think about that anymore.

Cecily

I've been watching the homeless woman they call Gracie for two years now, ever since I left my husband and moved into the studio over the Lucky Shamrock and started to write my novel. She shows up every morning promptly at nine and sits next to the mail-storage box and holds court with the pigeons. People in the neighborhood bring her food, and she always shares it with the birds. You'd expect them to flock all over her, but instead they hang back respectfully, each waiting its turn. It's as if Gracie and they speak the same language, although I've never heard her say a word to them.

How to describe her without relying on the obvious stereotypes of homeless persons? Not that she isn't stereotypical: She's ragged and she smells bad and her gray-brown hair is long and tangled. But in spite of the wrinkles and roughness of her skin, she seems ageless, and on days like this when she smiles and turns her face up to the sun she has a strange kind of beauty. Beauty disrupted by what I take to be flashes of pain. Not physical, but psychic pain—the reason, perhaps, that she took up residence on the cracked sidewalk of the Mission District.

I wish I knew more about her.

All I know are these few things: She's somewhere in her late thirties, a few years older than I. She told the corner grocer that. She has what she calls a "hidey-hole" where she goes to sleep at night—someplace safe, she told the mailman, where she won't be disturbed. She guards her shopping cart full of plastic bags very carefully; she'd kill anyone who touched it, she warned my landlord. She's been coming here nearly four years and hasn't missed a single day; Deirdre, the bartender at the Lucky Shamrock, has kept track. She was born in Oroville, up in the foothills of the Sierras; she mentioned that to my neighbor when she saw him wearing a sweatshirt saying OROVILLE—BEST LITTLE CITY BY A DAM SITE.

And that's it.

Maybe there's a way to find out more about her. Amateur detective work. Call it research, if I feel a need to justify it. Gracie might make a good character for a story. Anyway, it would be something to fool around with while I watch the mailbox and listen for the phone, hoping somebody's going to buy my damn novel. Something to keep my mind off this endless cycle of hope and rejection. Something to keep my mind off my regrets.

Yes, maybe I'll try to find out more about Gracie.

Gracie

Today I'm studying on the cracks in the sidewalk. They're pretty compli-
cated, running this way and that, and on the surface they look dark and
empty. But if you got down real close and put your eye to them there's no
telling what you might see. In a way the cracks're like people. Or music.
Music . . .
Nope, that's something else I can't think about.
Seems the list of what I can't think on is getting longer and longer. Bits
of the past tug at me, and then I've got to push them away. Like soft
summer nights when it finally cools and the lawn sprinklers twirl on the
grass. Like the sleepy eyes of a little boy when you tuck him into bed. Like
the feel of a guitar in your hands.
My hands.
My little boy.
Soft summer nights up in Oroville.
No.
Forget the cracks, Gracie. There's that woman again—the one with the
curly red hair and green eyes that're always watching. Watching *you*. Talk-
ing about you to the folks in the stores and the restaurants. Wonder what
she wants?
Not my cart—it better not be my cart. My gold's in there.
My gold . . .
No. That's at the top of the list.

Cecily

By now I've spoken with everybody in the neighborhood who's had any
contact with Gracie, and only added a few details to what I already know.
She hasn't been back to Oroville for over ten years, and she never will go
back; somebody there did a "terrible thing" to her. When she told that to
my neighbor, she became extremely agitated and made him a little afraid.
He thought she might be about to tip over into a violent psychotic episode,
but the next time he saw her she was as gentle as ever. Frankly, I think
he's making too much of her rage. He ought to see the heap of glass I had
to sweep off my kitchenette floor yesterday when yet another publisher
returned my manuscript.
Gracie's also quite familiar with the Los Angeles area—she demonstrated
that in several random remarks she made to Deirdre. She told at least three
people that she came to San Francisco because the climate is mild and she
knew she'd have to live on the street. She sings to the pigeons sometimes,
very low, and stops right away when she realizes somebody's listening. My

landlord's heard her a dozen times or more, and he says she's got a good voice. Oh, yes—she doesn't drink or do drugs. She told one of the waiters at Gino's that she has to keep her mind clear so she can control it—whatever that means.

Not much to go on. I wish I could get a full name for her; I'm not even sure Gracie *is* her name. God, I'm glad to have this little project to keep me occupied! Disappointments pile on disappointments lately, and sometimes I feel as if I were trapped in one of those cracks in the sidewalk that obviously fascinate Gracie. As if I'm being squeezed tighter and tighter . . .

Enough of that. I think I'll go to the library and see if they have that book on finding people that I heard about. Technically, Gracie isn't lost, but her identity's missing. Maybe the book would give me an idea of how to go about locating it.

Gracie

Not feeling so good today, I don't know why, and that red-haired woman's snooping around again. Who the hell is she? A fan?

Yeah, sure. A fan of old Gracie. Old Gracie, who smells bad and has got the look of a loser written all over her.

House of cards, he used to say. It can all collapse at any minute, and then how'll you feel about your sacrifices? *Sacrifices.* The way he said it, it sounded like a filthy word. But I never gave up anything that mattered. Well, one thing, one person—but I didn't know I was giving him up at the time.

No, no, *no*!

The past's tugging at me more and more, and I don't seem able to push it away so easy. Control, Gracie. But I'm not feeling good, and I think it's gonna rain. Another night in my hidey-hole with the rain beating down, trying not to remember the good times. The high times. The times when—

No.

Cecily

What a joke my life is. Three thanks-but-no-thanks letters from agents I'd hoped would represent me, and I can't even get the Gracie project off the ground. The book I checked out of the library was about as helpful—as my father used to say—as tits on a billygoat. Not that it wasn't informative and thorough. Gracie's just not a good subject for that kind of investigation.

I tried using the data sheet in the appendix. Space at the top for name: Gracie. Also known as: ? Last known address: Oroville, California—but that was more than ten years ago. Last known phone number: ? Automobiles owned, police record, birth date, Social Security number, real estate owned, driver's license number, profession, children, relatives, spouse: all blank. Height: five feet six, give or take. Weight: too damn thin. Present location: divides time between postal storage box 27368 and hidey-hole, location unknown.

Some detective, me.

Give it up, Cecily. Give it up and get on with your life. Take yourself downtown to the temp agency and sign on for a three-month job before your cash all flows out. Better yet, get yourself a real, permanent job and give up your stupid dreams. They aren't going to happen.

But they might. Wasn't I always one of the lucky ones? Besides, they tell you that all it takes is one editor who likes your work. They tell you all it takes is keeping at it. A page a day, and in a year you'll have a novel. One more submission, and soon you'll see your name on a book jacket. And there's always the next manuscript. This Gracie would make one hell of a character, might even make the basis for a good novel. If only I could find out . . .

The cart. Bet there's something in that damned cart that she guards so carefully. Tomorrow I think I'll try to befriend Gracie.

Gracie

Feeling real bad today, even my pigeons sense it and leave me alone. That red-haired woman's been sneaking around. This morning she brought me a bagel slathered in cream cheese just the way I like them. I left the bagel for the pigeons, fed the cream cheese to a stray cat. I know a bribe when I see one.

Bribes. There were plenty: a new car if you're a good girl. A new house, too, if you cooperate. And there was the biggest bribe of all, the one they never came through with. . . .

No.

Funny, things keep misting over today, and I'm not even crying. Haven't cried for years. No, this reminds me more of the smoky neon haze and the flashing lights. The sea of faces that I couldn't pick a single individual out of. Smoky sea of faces, but it didn't matter. The one I wanted to see wasn't there.

Bribes, yeah. Lies, really. *We'll make sure everything's worked out. Trust us. It's taking longer than we thought. He's making it difficult. Be patient. And by the way, we're not too sure about this new material.*

Bribes . . .
The wall between me and the things on my list of what not to remember is crumbling. Where's my control? That wall's my last defense. . . .

Cecily

Deirdre's worried about Gracie. She's looking worse than usual and has been refusing food. She fed the bagel I brought her to the pigeons, even though Del at Gino's said bagels with cream cheese are one of her favorite things. Deirdre thinks we should do something—but what?

Notify her family? Not possible. Take her to a hospital? She's not likely to have health insurance. I suppose there's always a free clinic, but would she agree to go? I doubt it. There's no doubt she's shutting out the world, though. She barely acknowledges anyone.

I think I'll follow her to her hidey-hole tonight. We ought to know where it is, in case she gets seriously ill. Besides, maybe there's a clue to who she is secreted there.

Gracie

The pigeons've deserted me, guess they know I'm not really with them anymore. I'm mostly back there in the smoky neon past and the memories're really pulling hard now. The unsuspecting look on my little boy's face and the regret in my heart when I tucked him in, knowing it was the last time. The rage on his father's face when I said I was leaving. The lean times that weren't really so lean because I sure wasn't living like I am today. The high times that didn't last. The painful times when I realized they weren't going to keep their promises.

It'll be all right. We'll arrange everything.

But it wasn't all right and nothing got arranged. It'll never be all right again.

Cecily

Gracie's hidey-hole is an abandoned trash Dumpster behind a condemned building on 18th Street. I had quite a time finding it. The woman acts like a criminal who's afraid she's being tailed, and it took three nights of ducking into doorways and hiding behind parked cars to follow her there. I watched through a hole in the fence while she unloaded the plastic bags from her cart to the Dumpster, then climbed in after them. The clang when she pulled the lid down was deafening, and I can imagine how noisy it is in there when it rains, like it's starting to right now. Anyway, Gracie's home for the night.

Tomorrow morning after she leaves I'm going to investigate that Dumpster.

Gracie

Rain thundering down hard, loud and echoing like applause. It's the only applause old Gracie's likely to hear anymore.

Old Gracie, that's how I think of myself. And I'm only thirty-nine, barely middle-aged. But I crammed a lot into those last seventeen years, and life catches up with some of us faster than others. I don't know as I'd have the nerve to look in a mirror anymore. What I'd see might scare me.

That red-haired woman was following me for a couple of nights—after my gold, for sure—but today I didn't see her. How she knows about the gold, I don't know. I never told anybody, but that must be it, it's all I've got of value. I'm gonna have to watch out for her, but keeping on guard is one hell of a job when you're feeling like I do.

It must be the rain. If only this rain'd stop, I'd feel better.

Cecily

Checking out that Dumpster was about the most disgusting piece of work I've done in years. It smelled horrible, and the stench is still with me—in my hair and on my clothing. The bottom half is covered with construction debris like two-by-fours and Sheetrock, and on top of it Gracie's made a nest of unbelievably filthy bedding. At first I thought there wasn't anything of hers there and, frankly, I wasn't too enthusiastic about searching thoroughly. But then, in a space between some planking beneath the wad of bedding, I found a cardboard gift box—heart-shaped and printed with roses that had faded almost to white. Inside it were some pictures of a little boy.

He was a chubby little blond, all dressed up to have his photo taken, and on the back of each somebody had written his name—Michael Joseph—and the date. In one he wore a party hat and had his hand stuck in a birthday cake, and on its back was the date—March 8, 1975—and his age—two years.

Gracie's little boy? Probably. Why else would she have saved his pictures and the lock of hair in the blue envelope that was the only other thing in the box?

So now I have a lead. A woman named Gracie (if that's her real name) had a son named Michael Joseph on March 8, 1973, perhaps in Oroville. Is that enough information to justify a trip up to Butte County to check the birth records? A trip in my car, which by all rights shouldn't make it to the San Francisco county line?

Well, why not? I collected yet another rejection letter yesterday. I need to get away from here.

Gracie

I could tell right away when I got back tonight—somebody's been in my hidey-hole. Nothing looked different, but I could smell whoever it was, the way one animal can smell another.

I guess that's what it all boils down to in the end: We're not much different from the animals.

I'll stay here tonight because it's raining again and I'm weary from the walk and unloading my cart. But tomorrow I'm out of here. Can't stay where it isn't safe. Can't sleep in a place somebody's defiled.

Well, they didn't find anything. Everything I own was in my cart. Everything except the box with the pictures of Mikey. They disappeared a few years ago, right about the time I moved in here. Must've fallen out of the cart, or else somebody took them. Doesn't matter, though; I remember him as clear as if I'd tucked him in for the last time only yesterday. Remember his father, too, cursing me as I went out the door, telling me I'd never see my son again.

I never did.

I remember all the promises, too; my lawyer and my manager were going to work it all out so I could have Mikey with me. But his father made it difficult and then things went downhill and then there was the drug bust and all the publicity—

Why am I letting the past suck me in? All those years I had such good control. No more drink, no more drugs, just pure, strong control. A dozen years on the street, first down south, then up here, and I always kept my mind on the present and its tiny details. My pigeons, the people passing by, the cracks in the sidewalk . . .

It's like I've tumbled into one of those cracks. I'm falling and I don't know what'll happen next.

Cecily

Here I am in Oroville, in a cheap motel not far from the Butte County Courthouse. By all rights I shouldn't have made it this far. The car tried to die three times—once while I was trying to navigate the freeway maze at Sacramento—but I arrived before the vital statistics department closed. And now I know who Gracie is!

Michael Joseph Venema was born on March 8, 1973, to Michael William and Grace Ann Venema in Butte Hospital. The father was thirty-five at the time, the mother only sixteen. Venema's not a common name here; the current directory lists only one—initial *M*—on Lark Lane. I've already located it on the map, and I'm going there tomorrow morning. It's a Saturday, so somebody's bound to be at home. I'll just show up and maybe the element of surprise will help me pry loose the story of my neighborhood bag lady.

God, I'm good at this! Maybe I should scrap my literary ambitions and become an investigative reporter.

Gracie

I miss my Dumpster. Was noisy when it rained, that's true, but at least it was dry. The only shelter I could find tonight was this doorway behind Gino's, and I had to wait for them to close up before I crawled into it, so I got plenty wet. My blankets're soaked, but the plastic has to go over my cart to protect my things. How much longer till morning?

Well, how would I know? Haven't had a watch for years. I pawned it early on, that was when I was still sleeping in hotel rooms, thinking things would turn around for me. Then I was sleeping in my car and had to sell everything else, one by one. And then it was a really cheap hotel, and I turned some tricks to keep the money coming, but when a pimp tried to move in on me, I knew it was time to get my act together and leave town. So I came here and made do. In all the years I've lived on the street in different parts of this city, I've never turned another trick and I've never panhandled. For a while before I started feeling so bad I picked up little jobs, working just for food. But lately I've had to rely on other people's kindnesses.

It hurts to be so dependent.

There's another gust of wind, blowing the rain at me. It's raining like a son of a bitch tonight. It better let up in the morning.

I miss my Dumpster. I miss . . .

No. I've still got *some* control left. Not much, but a shred.

Cecily

Now I know Gracie's story, and I'm so distracted that I got on the wrong freeway coming back through Sacramento. There's a possibility I may be able to reunite her with her son Mike—plus I've got my novel, all of it, and it's going to be terrific! I wouldn't be surprised if it changed my life.

I went to Mike's house this morning—a little prefab on a couple of acres in the country south of town. He was there, as were his wife and baby son. At first he didn't believe his mother was alive, then he didn't want to talk about her. But when I told him Gracie's circumstances he opened up and agreed to tell me what he knew. And he knew practically everything, because his father finally told him the truth when he was dying last year.

Gracie was a singer. One of those bluesy-pop kind like Linda Ronstadt, whom you can't categorize as either country or Top 40. She got her start singing at their church and received some encouragement from a friend's uncle who was a sound engineer at an L.A. recording studio. At sixteen she'd married Mike's father—who was nearly twenty years her senior—and they'd never been very happy. So on the strength of that slim encouragement, she left him and their son and went to L.A. to try to break into the business.

And she did, under the name Grace Ventura. The interesting thing is, I remember her first hit, "Smoky Neon Haze," very clearly. It was romantic and tragic, and I was just at the age when tragedy is an appealing concept rather than a harsh reality.

Anyway, Mike's father was very bitter about Gracie deserting them—the way my husband was when I told him I was leaving to become a writer. After Gracie's first album did well and her second earned her a gold record, she decided she wanted custody of Mike, but there was no way his father would give him up. Her lawyer initiated a custody suit, but while that was going on Gracie's third album flopped. Gracie started drinking and doing drugs and couldn't come up with the material for a fourth album; then she was busted for possession of cocaine, and Mike's father used that against her to gain permanent custody. And then the record company dropped her. She tried to make a comeback for a couple of years, then finally disappeared. She had no money; she'd signed a contract that gave most of her earnings to the record label, and what they didn't take, her manager and lawyer did. No wonder she ended up on the streets.

I'm not sure how Mike feels about being reunited with his mother; he was very noncommittal. He has his own life now, and his printing business is just getting off the ground. But he did say he'd try to help her, and that's the message I'm to deliver to Gracie when I get back to the city.

I hope it works out. For Gracie's sake, of course, and also because it would make a perfect upbeat ending to my novel.

Gracie

It's dry and warm here in the storage room. Deirdre found me crouched behind the garbage cans in the alley a while ago and brought me inside. Gave me some blankets she borrowed from one of the folks upstairs. They're the first clean things I've had next to my skin in years.

Tomorrow she wants to take me to the free clinic. I won't go, but I'm grateful for the offer.

Warm and dry and dark in here. I keep drifting—out of the present, into the past, back and forth. No control now. In spite of the dark I can see the lights—bright colors, made hazy by the smoke. Just like in that first song . . . what was it called? Don't remember. Doesn't matter.

It was a good one, though. Top of the charts. Didn't even surprise me. I always thought I was one of the lucky ones.

I can see the faces, too. Seems like acres of them, looking up at me while I'm blinded by the lights. Listen to the applause! For me. And that didn't surprise me, either. I always knew it would happen. But where was that? When?

Can't remember. Doesn't matter.

Was only one face that ever mattered. Little boy. Who was he?

Michael Joseph. Mikey.

Funny, for years I've fought the memories. Pushed them away when they tugged, kept my mind on the here and now. Then I fell into the crack in the sidewalk, and it damn near swallowed me up. Now the memories're fading, except for one. Michael Joseph. Mikey.

That's a good one. I'll hold on to it.

Cecily

Gracie died last night in the storeroom at the Lucky Shamrock. Deirdre brought her in there to keep her out of the rain, and when she looked in on her after closing, she was dead. The coroner's people said it was pneumonia; she'd probably been walking around with it for a long time, and the soaking finished her.

I cried when Deirdre told me. I haven't cried in years, and there I was, sobbing over a woman whose full name I didn't even know until two days ago.

I wonder why she wasn't in her hidey-hole. Was it because she realized I violated it and didn't feel safe anymore? God, I hope not! But how could she have known?

I wish I could've told her about her son, that he said he'd help her. But maybe it's for the best, after all. Gracie might have wanted more than Mike was willing to give her—emotionally, I mean. Besides, she must've been quite unbalanced toward the end.

I guess it's for the best, but I still wish I could've told her.

This morning Deirdre and I decided we'd better go through the stuff in her cart, in case there was anything salvageable that Mike might want. Some of the plastic bags were filled with ragged clothing, others with faded and crumbling clippings that chronicled the brief career of Grace Ventura. There was a Bible, some spangled stage costumes, a few paperbacks, a bundle of letters about the custody suit, a set of keys to a Mercedes, and other mementos that were in such bad shape we couldn't tell what they'd been. But at the very bottom of the cart, wrapped in rags and more plastic bags, was the gold record awarded to her for her second album, "Soft Summer Nights."

On one hand, not much to say for a life that once held such promise. On the other hand, it says it all.

It gives me pause. Makes me wonder about my own life. Is all of this worth it? I really don't know. But I'm not giving up—not now, when I've got Gracie's story to tell. I wouldn't be the least bit surprised if it changed my life.

After all, aren't I one of the lucky ones?

Aren't I?

The no-nonsense lawyer Laura Di Palma is the creation of Lia Matera, who has written several novels about her, the most recent being *Designer Crimes*. Her other series character is Willa Jansson, another California attorney whose approach to life is a little more laid back. Here she combines elements of both characters in a third lawyer who discovers a different side of life and death on skid row.

Dead Drunk
LIA MATERA

My secretary, Jan, asked if I'd seen the newspaper: another homeless man had frozen to death. I frowned up at her from my desk. Her tone said *And you think you've got problems?*

My secretary is a paragon. I would not have a law practice without her. I would have something resembling my apartment, which looks like a college crash pad. But I have to cut Jan a lot of slack. She's got a big personality.

Not that she actually says anything. She doesn't have to, any more than earthquakes bother saying "shake shake."

"Froze?" I murmured. I shoved documents around the desk, knowing she wouldn't take the hint.

"Froze to death. This is the fourth one. They find them in the parks, frozen."

"It has been cold," I agreed.

"You really haven't been reading the papers!" Her eyes went on highbeam. "They're wet, that's why they freeze."

She sounded mad at me. Line forms on the right, behind my creditors.

"Must be the tule fog?" I guessed. I've never been sure what tule fog is. I didn't know if actual tules were required.

"You have been in your own little world lately. They've all been passed out drunk. Someone pours water over them while they lie there. It's been so cold, they end up frozen. To death."

I wondered if I could get away with, *How terrible*. Not that I didn't

51

think it was terrible. But Jan picks at what I say, looking for hidden sarcasm.

She leaned closer, as titillated as I'd ever seen her. "And here's the kicker. They went and analyzed the water on the clothes. It's got no chlorine in it—it's not tap water. It's bottled water! Imagine that. Perrier or Evian or something. Can you imagine? Somebody going out with expensive bottled water on purpose to pour it over passed-out homeless men." Her long hair fell over her shoulders. With her big glasses and serious expression, she looked like the bread-baking, natural foods mom that she was. "You know, it probably takes three or four bottles."

"What a murder weapon."

"It is murder." She sounded defensive. "Being wet drops the body temperature so low it kills them. In this cold, within hours."

"That's what I said."

"But you were . . . anyway, it is murder."

"I wonder if it has to do with the ordinance."

Our town had passed a no-camping ordinance that was supposed to chase the homeless out of town. If they couldn't sleep here, the theory went, they couldn't live here. But the city had too many parks to enforce the ban. What were cops supposed to do? Wake up everyone they encountered? Take them to jail and give them a warmer place to sleep?

"Of course it has to do with the ordinance! This is some asshole's way of saying, if you sleep here, you die here."

"Maybe it's a temperance thing. You know, don't drink."

"I know what temperance means." Jan could be touchy. She could be a lot of things, including a fast typist willing to work cheap. "I just don't believe the heartlessness of it, do you?"

I had to be careful; I did believe the heartlessness of it. "It's uncondonable," I agreed.

Still she stooped over my desk. There was something else.

"The guy last night," Jan said bitterly, "was laid off by Hinder. Years ago, but even so."

Hinder was the corporation Jan had been fired from before I hired her. She straightened. "I'm going to go give money to the guys outside."

"Who's outside?" Not my creditors?

"You are so oblivious. Linda! Homeless people, right downstairs. Regulars."

She was looking at me like I should know their names. I tried to look apologetic.

Ten minutes later, she buzzed me to say there was someone in the reception area. "He wants to know if you can fit him in."

That was our code for, *He looks legit.* We were not in the best neighborhood. We got our share of walk-ins with generalized grievances and a desire to vent at length and for free. For them, our code was, "I've told him you're busy."

"Okay."

A moment later, a kid—well, maybe young man, maybe even twenty-five or so—walked in. He was good-looking, well dressed, but too trendy, which is why he'd looked so young. He had the latest hairstyle, razored in places and long in others. He had running shoes that looked like inflatable pools.

He said, "I think I need a good lawyer."

My glance strayed to my walls, where my diploma announced I'd gone to a night school. I had two years' experience, some of it with no caseload. I resisted the urge to say, *Let me refer you to one.*

Instead, I asked, "What's the nature of your problem?"

He sat on my client chair, checking it first. I guess it was clean enough.

"I think I'm going to be arrested." He glanced at me a little sheepishly, a little boastfully. "I said something kind of stupid last night."

If that were grounds, they'd arrest me, too.

"I was at the Club," a fancy bar downtown. "I got a little tanked. A little loose." He waggled his shoulders.

I waited. He sat forward. "Okay, I've got issues." His face said, *Who wouldn't?* "I work my butt off."

I waited some more.

"Well, it burns me. I have to work for my money; I don't get welfare, I don't get free meals and free medicine and a free place to live." He shifted on the chair. "I'm not saying kill them. But it's unfair I have to pay for them."

"For who?"

"The trolls, the bums."

I was beginning to get it. "What did you say in the bar?"

"That I bought out Costoo's Perrier." He flushed to the roots of his chi-chi hair. "That I wish I'd thought of using it."

"On the four men?"

"I was high, okay?" he continued in a rush. "But then this morning, the cops come over." Tears sprang to his eyes. "They scared my mom. She took them out to see the water in the garage."

"You really did buy a lot of Perrier?"

"Just to drink! The police said they got a tip on their hot line. Someone at the bar told them about me. That's got to be it."

I nodded like I knew about the hot line.

"Now"—his voice quavered—"they've started talking to people where I work. Watch me get fired!"

Gee, buddy, then you'll qualify for free medical. "What would you like me to do for you, Mr. . . . ?"

"Kyle Kelly." He didn't stick out his hand. "Are they going to arrest me or what? I think I need a lawyer."

MY PRIVATE INVESTIGATOR WAS PISSED off at me. My last two clients hadn't paid me enough to cover his fees. It was my fault; I hadn't asked for enough in advance. Afterward, they'd stiffed me.

Now the PI was taking a hard line: he wouldn't work on this case until he got paid for the last two.

So I made a deal. I'd get his retainer from Kelly up front. I'd pay him for the investigation, but I'd do most of it myself. For every hour I investigated and he got paid, he'd knock an hour off what I owed him.

I wouldn't want the state bar to hear about the arrangement. But the parts that were on paper would look okay.

It meant I had a lot of legwork to do.

I started by driving to a park where two of the dead men were found. It was a chilly afternoon, with the wind whipping off the plains, blowing dead leaves over footpaths and lawns.

I wandered, looking for the spots described in police reports. The trouble was, every half-bare bush near lawn and benches looked the same. And many were decorated with detritus: paper bags, liquor bottles, discarded clothing.

As I was leaving the park, I spotted two paramedics squatting beside an addled-looking man. His clothes were stiff with dirt, his face covered in thick gray stubble. He didn't look wet. If anything, I was shivering more than him.

I watched the younger of the two paramedics shake his head, scowling, while the older talked at some length to the man. The man nodded, kept on nodding. The older medic showed him a piece of paper. The man nodded some more. The younger one strode to an ambulance parked on a nearby fire trail. It was red on white with "4–12" stenciled on the side.

I knew from police reports that paramedics had been called to pick up the frozen homeless men. Were they conducting an investigation of their own?

A minute later, the older medic joined his partner in the ambulance. It drove off.

The homeless man lay down, curling into a fetal position on the lawn, collar turned up against the wind.

I approached him cautiously. "Hi," I said. "Are you sick?"

"No!" He sat up again. "What's every damn body want to know if I'm sick for? 'Man down.' So what? What's a man got to be up about?"

He looked bleary-eyed. He reeked of alcohol and urine and musk. He was so potent, I almost lost my breakfast.

"I saw medics here talking to you. I thought you might be sick."

"Hassle hassle." He waved me away. When I didn't leave, he rose. "Wake us up, make us sign papers."

"What kind of papers?"

"Don't want to go to the hospital." His teeth were in terrible condition. I tried not to smell his breath. "Like I want yelling from the nurses, too."

"What do they yell at you about?"

"Cost them money; I'm costing everybody money. Yeah, well, maybe they should have thought of that before they put my-Johnny-self in the helicopter. Maybe they should have left me with the rest of the platoon."

He lurched away from me. I could see that one leg was shorter than the other.

I went back to my car. I was driving past a nearby sandwich shop when I saw ambulance 4–12 parked there. I pulled into the space behind it.

I went into the shop. The medics were sitting at a small table, looking bored. They were hard to miss in their cop-blue uniforms and utility belts hung with flashlights, scissors, tape, stethoscopes.

I walked up to them. "Hi," I said. "Do you mind if I talk to you for a minute?"

The younger one looked through me; no one's ever accused me of being pretty. The older one said, "What about?"

"I'm representing a suspect in the . . ." I hated to call it what the papers were now calling it, but it was the best shorthand. "The Perrier murders. Of homeless men."

That got the younger man's attention. "We knew those guys," he said.

"My client didn't do it. But he could get arrested. Do you mind helping me out? Telling me a little about them?"

They glanced at each other. The younger man shrugged.

"We saw them all the time. Every time someone spotted them passed out and phoned in a 'man down' call, we'd code-three it out to the park or the tracks or wherever."

The older paramedic gestured for me to sit. "Hard times out there. We've got a lot more regulars than we used to."

I sat down. The men, I noticed, were lingering over coffee. "I just saw you in the park."

"Lucky for everybody, my-Johnny-self was sober enough to AMA." The younger man looked irritated. " 'Against medical advice.' We get these calls all the time. Here we are a city's got gang wars going on, knifings, drive-bys, especially late at night; and we're diddling around with passed-out drunks who want to be left alone anyway."

The older man observed, "Ben's new, still a hot dog, wants every call to be the real deal."

"Yeah, well, what a waste of effort, Dirk," the younger man, Ben, shot back. "We get what? Two, three, four man-down calls a day. We have to respond to every one. It could be some poor diabetic, right, or a guy's had a heart attack. But you get out there, and it's some alcoholic. If he's too out of it to tell us he's just drunk, we have to transport and work him up. Which he doesn't want—he wakes up pissed off at having to hoof it back to the park. Or worse, with the new ordinance, he gets arrested."

"Ridiculous ordinance," the older medic interjected.

"And it's what, maybe five or six hundred dollars the company's out of pocket?" his partner continued. "Not to mention that everybody's time gets totally wasted, and maybe somebody with a real emergency's out there waiting for us. Your grandmother could be dying of a heart attack while we play taxi. It's bullshit."

"It's all in a night's work, Ben." Dirk looked at me. "You start this job, you want every call to be for real. But you do it a few years, you get to know your regulars. Clusters of them near the liquor stores; you could draw concentric circles around each store and chart the man-down calls, truly. But what are you going to do? Somebody sees a man lying in the street or in the park, they've got to call, right? And if the poor bastard's too drunk to tell us he's fine, we can't just leave him. It's our license if we're wrong."

"They should change the protocols," Ben insisted. "If we know who they are, if we've run them in three, four, even ten times, we should be able to leave them to sleep it off."

Dirk said, "You'd get lawsuits."

"So these guys either stiff the company or welfare picks up the tab, meaning you and me pay the five hundred bucks. It offends logic."

"So you knew the men who froze." I tried to get back on track. "Did you pick them up when they died?"

"I went on one of the calls," Ben said defensively. "Worked him up."

"Sometimes with hypothermia," Dirk added, "body functions slow down so you can't really tell if they're dead till they warm up. So we'll spend, oh God, an hour or more doing CPR. Till they're warm and dead."

"While people wait for an ambulance somewhere else," Ben repeated.

"You'll mellow out," Dirk promised. "For one thing, you see them year in, year out, you stop being such a hard-ass. Another thing, you get older, you feel more sympathy for how hard the street's got to be on the poor bones."

Ben's beeper went off. He immediately lifted it out of his utility belt, pressing a button and filling the air with static. A voice cut through: "Unit four-twelve, we have a possible shooting at Kins and Booten streets."

The paramedics jumped up, saying " 'Bye" and "Gotta go," as they strode past me and out the door. Ben, I noticed, was smiling.

*   *   *

MY NEXT STOP WAS JUST a few blocks away. It was a rundown stucco building that had recently been a garage, a factory, a cult church, a rehab center, a magic shop. Now it was one of the few homeless shelters in town. I thought the workers there might have known some of the dead men.

I was ushered in to see the director, a big woman with a bad complexion. When I handed her my card and told her my business, she looked annoyed.

"Pardon me, but your client sounds like a real shit."

"I don't know him well enough to judge," I admitted. "But he denies doing it, and I believe him. And if he didn't do it, he shouldn't get blamed. You'd agree with that?"

"Some days," she conceded. She motioned me to sit in a scarred chair opposite a folding-table desk. "Other days, tell the truth, I'd round up all the holier-than-thou jerks bitching about the cost of a place like this, and I'd shoot 'em. Christ, they act like we're running a luxury hotel here. Did you get a look around?"

I'd seen women and children and a few old men on folding chairs or duck-cloth cots. I hadn't seen any food.

"It's enough to get your goat," the director continued. "The smugness, the condemnation. And ironically, how many paychecks away from the street do you think most people are? One? Two?"

"Is that mostly who you see here? People who got laid off?"

She shrugged. "Maybe half. We get a lot of people who are frankly just too tweaked-out to work. What can you do? You can't take a screwdriver and fix them. No use blaming them for it."

"Did you know any of the men who got killed?"

She shook her head. "No, no. We don't take drinkers, we don't take anybody under the influence. We can't. Nobody would get any sleep, nobody would feel safe. Alcohol's a nasty drug, lowers inhibitions; you get too much attitude, too much noise. We can't deal with it here. We don't let in anybody we think's had a drink, and if we find alcohol, we kick the person out. It's that simple."

"What recourse do they have? Drinkers, I mean."

"Sleep outside. They want to sleep inside, they have to stay sober, no ifs, ands, or buts."

"The camping ban makes that illegal."

"Well," she said tartly, "it's not illegal to stay sober."

"You don't view it as an addiction?"

"There's AA meetings five times a night at three locations." She ran a hand through her already-disheveled hair. "I'm sorry, but it's a struggle scraping together money to take care of displaced families in this town. Then you've got to contend with people thinking you're running some kind of flophouse for drunks. Nobody's going to donate money for that."

I felt a twinge of pity. No room at the inn for alcoholics, and not much sympathy from paramedics. Now, someone—please God, not my client—was dousing them so they'd freeze to death.

With the director's permission, I wandered through the shelter.

A young woman lay on a cot with a blanket over her legs. She was reading a paperback.

"Hi," I said. "I'm a lawyer. I'm working on the case of the homeless men who died in the parks recently. Do you know about it?"

She sat up. She looked like she could use a shower and a makeover, but she looked more together than most of the folks in there. She wasn't mumbling to herself, and she didn't look upset or afraid.

"Yup—big news here. And major topic on the street."

"Did you know any of the men?"

"I'll tell you what I've heard." She leaned forward. "It's a turf war."

"A turf war?"

"Who gets to sleep where, that kind of thing. A lot of crazies on the street, they get paranoid. They gang up on each other. Alumni from the closed-down mental hospitals. You'd be surprised." She pushed up her sleeve and showed me a scar. "One of them cut me."

"Do you know who's fighting whom?"

"Yes." Her eyes glittered. "Us women are killing off the men. They say we're out on the street for their pleasure, and we say, death to you, bozo."

I took a backward step, alarmed by the look on her face.

She showed me her scar again. "I carve a line for every one I kill." She pulled a tin St. Christopher out from under her shirt. "I used to be a Catholic. But Clint Eastwood is my god now."

I PULLED INTO A PARKING lot with four ambulances parked in a row. A sign on a two-story brick building read "Central Ambulance." I hoped they'd give me their records regarding the four men.

I smiled warmly at the front-office secretary. When I explained what I wanted, she handed me a records-request form. "We'll contact you within five business days regarding the status of your request."

If my client got booked, I could subpoena the records. So I might, unfortunately, have them before anyone even read this form.

As I sat there filling it out, a thin boy in a paramedic uniform strolled in. He wore his medic's bill cap backward. His utility belt was hung with twice the gadgets of the two men I'd talked to earlier. Something resembling a big rubber band dangled from his back pocket. I supposed it was a tourniquet, but on him it gave the impression of a slingshot.

He glanced at me curiously. He said, "Howdy, Mary," to the secretary.

She didn't look glad to see him. "What now?"

"Is Karl in?"

"No. What's so important?"

"I was thinking instead of just using the HEPA filters, if we—"

"Save it. I'm busy."

I shot him a sympathetic look. I know how it feels to be bullied by a secretary.

I handed her my request and walked out behind the spurned paramedic.

I was surprised to see him climb into a cheap Geo car. He was in uniform. I'd assumed he was working.

All four men had been discovered in the morning. It had probably taken them most of the night to freeze to death; they'd been picked up by ambulance in the wee hours. Maybe this kid could tell me who'd worked those shifts.

I tapped at his passenger window. He didn't hesitate to lean across and open the door. He looked alert and happy, like a curious puppy.

"Hi," I said. "I was wondering if you could tell me about your shifts? I was going to ask the secretary, but she's not very . . . friendly."

He nodded as if her unfriendliness were a fact of life, nothing to take personally. "Come on in. What do you want to know?" Then, more suspiciously, "You're not a lawyer?"

I climbed in quickly. "Well, yes, but—"

"Oh, man. You know, we do the very best we can." He whipped off his cap, rubbing his crewcut in apparent annoyance. "We give a hundred and ten percent."

I suddenly placed his concern. "No, no, it's not about medical malpractice, I swear."

He continued scowling at me.

"I represent a young man who's been falsely accused of—"

"You're not here about malpractice?"

"No, I'm not."

"Because that's such a crock." He flushed. "We work our butts off. Twelve-hour shifts, noon to midnight, and a lot of times we get forced-manned onto a second shift. If someone calls in sick or has to go out of service because they got bled all over or punched out, someone's got to hold over. When hell's a-poppin' with the gangs, we've got guys working forty-eights or even seventy-twos." He shook his head. "It's just plain unfair to blame us for everything that goes wrong. Field medicine's like combat conditions. We don't have everything all clean and handy like they do at the hospital."

"I can imagine. So you work—"

"And it's not like we're doing it for the money! Starting pay's eight-fifty an hour; it takes years to work up to twelve. Your garbage collector earns more than we do."

I was a little off balance. "Your shifts—"

"Because half our calls, nobody pays the bill—Central Ambulance is probably the biggest pro bono business in town. So we get stuck at eight-fifty an hour. For risking AIDS, hepatitis, TB."

I didn't want to get pulled into his grievances. "You work twelve-hour shifts? Set shifts?"

"Rotating. Sometimes you work the day half, sometimes the night half."

Rotating; I'd need schedules and rosters. "The guys who work midnight to noon, do they get most of the drunks?"

He shrugged. "Not necessarily. We've got 'em passing out all day long. It's never too early for an alcoholic to drink." He looked bitter. "I had one in the family," he complained. "I should know."

"Do you know who picked up the four men who froze to death?"

His eyes grew steely. "I'm not going to talk about the other guys. You'll have to ask the company." He started the car.

I contemplated trying another question, but he was already shifting into gear. I thanked him, and got out. As I closed the door, I noticed a bag in back with a Garry's Liquors logo. Maybe the medic had something in common with the four dead men.

But it wasn't just drinking that got those men into trouble. It was not having a home to pass out in.

I STOOD AT THE SPOT where police had found the fourth body. It was a small neighborhood park.

Just after sunrise, an early jogger had phoned 911 from his cell phone. A man had been lying under a hedge. He'd looked dead. He'd looked wet.

The police had arrived first, then firemen, who'd taken a stab at resuscitating him. Then paramedics had arrived to work him up and transport him to the hospital, where he was pronounced dead. I knew that much from today's newspaper.

I found a squashed area of grass where I supposed the dead man had lain yesterday. I could see pocks and scuffs where workboots had tramped. I snooped around. Hanging from a bush was a rubber tourniquet. A paramedic must have squatted with his back against the shrubbery.

Flung deeper into the brush was a bottle of whiskey. Had the police missed it? Not considered it evidence? Or had it been discarded since?

I stared at it, wondering. If victim number four hadn't already been pass-out drunk, maybe someone helped him along.

I stopped by Parsifal MiniMart, the liquor store nearest the park. If anyone knew the dead man, it would be the proprietor.

He nodded. "Yup. I knew every one of those four. What kills me is the papers act like they were nobodies, like that's what 'alcoholic' means." He was a tall, red-faced man, given to karate-chop gestures. "Well, they were pretty good guys. Not mean, not full of shit, just regular guys. Buddy was a little"—he wiggled his hand—"not right in the head; heard voices and all that, but not violent that I ever saw. Mitch was a good guy. One of those jocks who's a hero as a kid but then gets hooked on the booze. I'll tell ya, I wish I could have made every kid comes in here for beer spend the day with Mitch. Donnie and Bill were . . . how can I put this without sounding like a racist? You know, a lot of older black guys are hooked on something. Check out the neighborhood. You'll see groups of them talking jive and keeping the curbs warm."

Something had been troubling me. Perhaps this was the person to ask. "Why didn't they wake up when the cold water hit them?"

The proprietor laughed. "Those guys? If I had to guess, I'd say their blood alcohol was one-point-oh even when they weren't drinking, just naturally from living the life. Get enough Thunderbird in them, and you're talking practically a coma." He shook his head. "They were just drunks; I know we're not talking about killing Mozart here. But the attitude behind what happened—man, it's cold. Perrier, too. That really tells you something."

"I heard there was no chlorine in the water. I don't think they've confirmed a particular brand of water."

"I just saw on the news they arrested some kid looks like a fruit, one of those hairstyles." The proprietor shrugged. "He had a bunch of Perrier. Cases of it from a discount place—I guess he didn't want to pay full price. Guess it wasn't even worth a buck a bottle to him to freeze a drunk."

Damn, they'd arrested Kyle Kelly. Already.

"You don't know anything about a turf war, do you?" It was worth a shot. "Among the homeless?"

"Sure." He grinned. "The drunk sharks and the rummy jets." He whistled the opening notes of *West Side Story*.

I GOT TIED UP IN traffic. It was an hour later by the time I walked into the police station. My client was in an interrogation room by himself. When I walked in, he was crying.

"I told them I didn't do it." He wiped tears as if they were an embarrassing surprise. "But I was getting so tongue-tied. I told them I wanted to wait for you."

"I didn't think they'd arrest you, especially not so fast," I said. "You did exactly right, asking for me. I just wish I'd gotten here sooner. I wish I'd been in my office when you called."

He looked like he wished I had, too.

"All this over a bunch of bums," he marveled. "All the crime in this town, and they get hard-ons over winos!"

I didn't remind him that his own drunken bragging had landed him here. But I hope it occurred to him later.

* * *

I WAS SURROUNDED BY REPORTERS when I left the police station. They looked at me like my client had taken bites out of their children.

"Mr. Kelly is a very young person who regrets what alcohol made him say one evening. He bears no one any ill will, least of all the dead men, whom he never even met." I repeated some variation of this over and over as I battled my way to my car.

Meanwhile, their questions shed harsh light on my client's bragfest at the Club.

"Is it true he boasted about kicking homeless men and women?" "Is it true he said if homeless women didn't smell so bad, at least they'd be usable?" "Did he say three bottles of Perrier is enough, but four's more certain?" "Does he admit saying he was going to keep doing it till he ran out of Perrier?" "Is it true he once set a homeless man on fire?"

Some of the questions were just questions: "Why Perrier? Is it a statement?" "Why did he buy it in bulk?" "Is this his first arrest? Does he have a sealed juvenile record?"

I could understand why police had jumped at the chance to make an arrest. Reporters must have been driving them crazy.

After flustering me and making me feel like a laryngitic parrot, they finally let me through. I locked myself into my car and drove gratefully away. Traffic was good. It only took one half an hour to get back to the office.

I found the paramedic with the Geo parked in front. He jumped out of his car. "I just saw you on TV."

"What brings you here?"

"Well, I semi-volunteered, for the company newsletter. I mean, we picked up those guys a few times. It'd be good to put something into an article." He looked like one of those black-and-white sitcom kids. Opie or Timmy or someone. "I didn't quite believe you, before, about the malpractice. I'm sorry I was rude."

"You weren't rude."

"I just wasn't sure you weren't after us. Everybody's always checking up on everything we do. The nurses, the docs, our supervisors, other medics. Every patient care report gets looked at by four people. Our radio calls get monitored. Everybody jumps in our shit for every little thing."

I didn't have time to be Studs Terkel. "I'm sorry, I can't discuss my case with you."

"But I heard you say on TV your guy's innocent. You're going to get him off, right?" He gazed at me with a confidence I couldn't understand.

"Is that what you came here to ask?"

"It's just we knew those guys. I thought for the newsletter, if I wrote something . . ." He flushed. "Do you need information? You know, general stuff from a medical point of view?"

I couldn't figure him out. Why this need to keep talking to me about it? It was his day off; didn't he have a life?

But I *had* been wondering: "Why exactly do you carry those tourniquets? What do you do with them?"

He looked surprised. "We tie them around the arm to make a vein pop up. So we can start an intravenous line."

I glanced up at my office window, checking whether Jan had left. It was late; there were no more workers spilling out of buildings. A few derelicts lounged in doorways. I wondered if they felt safer tonight because someone had been arrested. With so many dangers on the street, I doubted it.

"Why would a tourniquet be in the bushes where the last man was picked up?" I hugged my briefcase. "I assumed a medic had dropped it, but you wouldn't start an intravenous line on a dead person, would you?"

"We don't do field pronouncements—pronounce them dead, I mean— in hypothermia cases. We leave that to the doc." He looked proud of himself, like he'd passed the pop quiz. "They're not dead till they're warm and dead."

"But why start an IV in this situation?"

"Get meds into them. If the protocols say to, we'll run a line even if we think they're deader than Elvis." He shrugged. "They warm up faster, too."

"What warms them up? What do you drip into them?"

"Epinephrine, atropine, normal saline. We put the saline bag on the dash to heat it as we drive—if we know we have a hypothermic patient."

"You have water in the units?"

"Of course."

"Special water?"

"Saline and distilled."

"Do you know a medic named Ben?"

He hesitated before nodding.

"Do you think he has a bad attitude about the homeless?"

"No more than you would," he protested. "We're the ones who have to smell them, have to handle them when they've been marinating in feces and urine and vomit. Plus they get combative at a certain stage. You do this disgusting waltz with them where they're trying to beat on you. And the smell is like, whoa. Plus if they scratch you, you can't help but be paranoid what they might infect you with."

"Ben said they cost your company money."

"They cost you and me money."

The look on his face scared me. Money's a big deal when you don't make enough of it.

I started past him.

He grabbed my arm. "Everything's breaking down." His tone was plaintive. "You realize that? Our whole society's breaking down. Everybody sees it—the homeless, the gangs, the diseases—but they don't have to deal with the physical results. They don't have to put their hands right on it, get all bloody and dirty with it, get infected by it."

"Let go!" I imagined being helpless and disoriented, a drunk at the mercy of a fed-up medic.

"And we don't get any credit"—he sounded angry now—"we just get checked up on." He gripped my arm tighter.

Again I searched my office window, hoping that Jan was still working, that I wasn't alone. But the office was dark.

A voice behind me said, "What you doin' to the lady, man?"

I turned to see a stubble-chinned black man in layers of rancid clothes. He'd stepped out of a recessed doorway. Even from here, I could smell alcohol.

"You let that lady go. You hear me?" He moved closer.

The medic's grip loosened.

The man might be drunk, but he was big. And he didn't look like he was kidding.

I jerked my arm free, backing toward him.

He said, "You're Jan's boss, aren't ya?"

"Yes." For the thousandth time, I thanked God for Jan. This must be one of the men she'd mother-henned this morning. "Thank you."

To the medic, I said, "The police won't be able to hold my client long. They've got to show motive and opportunity and no alibi on four different nights. I don't think they'll be able to do it. They were just feeling pressured to arrest someone. Just placating the media."

The paramedic stared behind me. I could smell the other man. I never thought I'd find the reek of liquor reassuring.

"Isn't that what your buddies sent you to find out? Whether they could rest easy, or if they'd screwed over an innocent person?"

The medic pulled his bill cap off, buffing his head with his wrist.

"Or maybe you decided on your own to come here. Your coworkers probably have sense enough to keep quiet and keep out of it. But you don't." He was young and enthusiastic; too much so, perhaps. "Well, you can tell Ben and the others not to worry about Kyle Kelly. His reputation's ruined for as long as people remember the name—which probably isn't long enough to teach him a lesson. But there's not enough evidence against him. He won't end up in jail because of you."

"Are you accusing *us* . . . ?" He looked more thrilled than shocked.

"Of dousing the men so you didn't have to keep picking them up? So you could respond to more important calls? Yes, I am."

"But who are you going to—-? What are you going to do?"

"I don't have a shred of proof to offer the police," I realized. "And I'm sure you guys will close ranks, won't give each other away. I'm sure the others will make you stop 'helping,' make you keep your mouth shut."

I thought about the dead men; "pretty good guys," according to the MiniMart proprietor. I thought about my-Johnny-self, the war veteran I'd spoken to this morning.

I wanted to slap this kid. Just to do *something*. "You know what? You need to be confronted with your arrogance, just like Kyle Kelly was. You need to see what other people think of you. You need to see some of your older, wiser coworkers look at you with disgust on their faces. You need your boss to rake you over the coals. You need to read what the papers have to say about you."

I could imagine headlines that sounded like movie billboards: "Dr. Death." "Central Hearse."

He winced. He'd done the profession no favor.

"So you can bet I'll tell the police what I think," I promised. "You can bet I'll try to get you fired, you and Ben and whoever else was involved. Even if there isn't enough evidence to arrest you."

He took a cautious step toward his car. "I didn't admit anything." He pointed to the other man. "Did you hear me admit anything?"

"And I'm sure your lawyer will tell you not to." If he could find a half-way decent one on his salary. "Now, if you'll excuse me, I have a lot of work to do."

I turned to the man behind me. "Would you mind walking me in to my office?" I had some cash inside. He needed it more than I did.

"Lead the way, little lady." His eyes were jaundiced yellow, but they were bright. I was glad he didn't look sick.

I prayed he wouldn't need an ambulance anytime soon.

Ed McBain has already achieved a status rarely attained in the mystery field. His gritty, sensitive 87th Precinct novels formed the basis for the police procedual story, and is still the benchmark series to which any others are compared. The exploits of Steve Carella and crew have spanned three decades and innumerable novels, each better than the last. Of course, writing about the law isn't the only thing he does. In "Running From Legs," he brings his inimitable style to a tale of Prohibition, gangsters, and love on the run in the 1930s.

Running From Legs
ED MCBAIN

Mahogany and brass.

Burnished and polished and gleaming under the green-shaded lights over the bar where men and women alike sat on padded stools and drank. Women, yes. In a saloon, yes. Sitting at the bar, and sitting in the black leather booths that lined the dimly lighted room. Women. Drinking alcohol. Discreetly, to be sure, for booze and speakeasies were against the law. Before Prohibition, you rarely saw a woman drinking in a saloon. Now you saw them in speakeasies all over the city. Where once there had been fifteen thousand bars, there were now thirty-two thousand speakeasies. The Prohibitionists hadn't expected these side effects of the Eighteenth Amendment.

The speakeasy was called the Brothers Three, named after Bruno Tataglia and his brothers Angelo and Mickey. It was located just off Third Avenue on 87th Street, in a part of the city named Yorkville after the Duke of York. We were here celebrating. My grandmother owned a chain of lingerie shops she called "Scanties," and today had been the grand opening of the third one. Her boyfriend Vinnie was with us, and so was Dominique Lefèvre, who worked for her in the second of her shops, the one on Lexington Avenue. My parents would have been here, too, but they'd been killed in an automobile accident while I was overseas.

In the other room, the band was playing "Ja-Da," a tune from the war years. We were all drinking from coffee cups. In the coffee cups was something very brown and very vile tasting, but it was not coffee.

Dominique was smiling.

It occurred to me that perhaps she was smiling at *me*.

Dominique was twenty-eight years old, a beautiful, dark-haired, dark-eyed woman, tall and slender and utterly desirable. A native of France, she had come to America as a widow shortly after the war ended; her husband had been killed three days before the guns went silent. One day, alone with her in my grandmother's shop—Dominique was folding silk panties, I was sitting on a stool in front of the counter, watching her—she told me she despaired of ever finding another man as wonderful as her husband had been. "I 'ave been spoil', *n'est-ce pas?*" she said. I adored her French accent. I told her that I, too, had suffered losses in my life. And so, like cautious strangers fearful of allowing even our *glances* to meet, we'd skirted the possibilities inherent in our chance proximity.

But now—her smile.

The Brothers Three was very crowded tonight. Lots of smoke and laughter and the sound of a four-piece band coming from the other room. Piano, drums, alto saxophone, and trumpet. There was a dance floor in the other room. I wondered if I should ask Dominique to dance. I had never danced with her. I tried to remember when last I'd danced with anyone.

I'd been limping, yes. And a French girl whispered in my ear—this was after I'd got out of the hospital, it was shortly after the armistice was signed—a French girl whispered to me in Paris that she found a man with a slight limp very sexy. *"Je trouve très séduisante,"* she said, *"une claudication légère."* She had nice *poitrines,* but I'm not sure I believed her. I think she was just being kind to an American doughboy who'd got shot in the foot during the fighting around the Bois des Loges on a bad day in November. I found that somewhat humiliating, getting shot in the foot. It did not seem very heroic, getting shot in the foot. I no longer limped, but I still had the feeling that some people thought I'd shot *myself* in the god-damn foot. To get out of the 78th Division or something. As if such a thought had ever crossed my mind.

Dominique kept smiling at me.

Boozily.

I figured she'd had too much coffee.

She was wearing basic black tonight. A simple black satin, narrow in silhouette, bare of back, its neckline square and adorned with pearls, its waistline low, its hemline falling to midthigh where a three-inch expanse of white flesh separated the dress from the rolled tops of her blond silk stockings. She was smoking. As were Vinnie and my grandmother. Smoking had something to do with drinking. If you drank, you smoked. That seemed to be the way it worked.

Dominique kept drinking and smoking and smiling at me.

I smiled back.

My grandmother ordered another round.

She was drinking Manhattans. Dominique was drinking Martinis. Vinnie was drinking something called a Between the Sheets, which was one-third brandy, one-third Cointreau, one-third rum, and a dash of lemon juice. I was drinking a Bosom Caresser. These were all cocktails, an American word made popular when drinking became illegal. Cocktails.

In the other room, a double paradiddle and a solid bassdrum shot ended the song. There was a pattering of applause, a slight expectant pause, and then the alto saxophone soared into the opening riff of a slow, sad, and bluesy rendition of "Who's Sorry Now?"

"Richard?" Dominique said, and raised one eyebrow. "Aren't you going to ask me to dance?"

She was easily the most beautiful woman in the room. Eyes lined with black mascara, lips and cheeks painted the color of all those poppies I'd seen growing in fields across the length and breadth of France. Her dark hair bobbed in a shingle cut, the scent of mimosa wafting across the table.

"Richard?"

Her voice a caress.

Alto saxophone calling mournfully from the next room.

Smoke swirling like fog coming in off the docks on the day we landed over there. We were back now because it was *over* over there. And I no longer limped. And Dominique was asking me to dance.

"Go dance with her," my grandmother said.

"Yes, come," Dominique said, and put out her cigarette. Rising, she moved out of the booth past my grandmother, who rescued her Manhattan by holding it close to her protective bosom, and then winked at me as if to say "These are new times, Richie, we have the vote now, we can drink and we can smoke, anything goes nowadays, Richie. Go dance with Dominique."

Is what my grandmother's wink seemed to say.

I took Dominique's hand.

Together, hand in hand, we moved toward the other room.

"I love this song," Dominique said, and squeezed my hand.

There were round tables with white tablecloths in the other room, embracing a half-moon-shaped, highly polished, parquet dance floor. The lights were dimmer in this part of the club, perhaps because the fox-trot was a new dance that encouraged cheeks against cheeks and hands upon asses. A party of three—a handsome man in a dinner jacket and two women in gowns—sat at one of the tables with Bruno Tataglia. Bruno was leaning over the table, in obviously obsequious conversation with the good-looking man whose eyes kept checking out women on the dance floor even though there was one beautiful woman sitting on his left and another on his right. Both women were wearing white satin gowns and they both had

purple hair. I had heard of women wearing orange, or red, or green, or
even purple wigs when they went out on the town, but this was the first
time I'd ever actually *seen* one.

Two, in fact.

I wondered how Dominique would look in a purple wig.

"Dominique?"

Bruno's voice.

He rose as we came abreast of the table, took her elbow, and said to the
man in the dinner jacket, "Mr. Noland, I'd like you to meet the beauteous
Dominique."

"Pleasure," Mr. Noland said.

Dominique nodded politely.

"And Richie here," Bruno said as an afterthought.

"Nice to meet you," I said.

Mr. Noland's eyes were on Dominique.

"Won't you join us?" he said.

"Thank you, but we're about to dance," Dominique said, and squeezed
my hand again, and led me out onto the floor. I held her close. We began
swaying in time to the music. The trumpet player was putting in a mute.
The piano player eased him into his solo.

Liquid brass.

Dominique's left hand moved up to the back of my neck.

"You dance well," she said.

"Thank you."

"Does it ever ache you? Your foot?"

"When it rains," I said.

"Was it terrible, the war?" she asked.

"Yes," I said.

I did not much feel like talking about it. I gently steered her away from
the ring of tables and back toward the bandstand, sweeping her gracefully
past the table where Bruno was grinning oleaginously at Mr. Noland and
his two blond bimbos.

Mr. Noland's eyes met mine.

A shiver ran up my spine.

I had never seen eyes like that in my life.

Not even on the battlefield.

Not even on men eager to kill me.

Dominique and I glided over the parquet floor.

Drifting, drifting to the sound of the muted horn.

There was a gentle tap on my shoulder.

I turned.

Mr. Noland was standing slightly behind me and slightly to my right,
his hand resting on my shoulder.

"I'm cutting in," he said.

And his hand tightened on my shoulder, and he moved me away from Dominique, my left hand still holding her right hand, and then stepped into the open circle his intrusion had created, looping his right arm around Dominique's waist and shouldering me out completely.

I moved clumsily off the dance floor and stood in the middle of the arch separating the two rooms, feeling somehow embarrassed and inadequate, watching helplessly as Mr. Noland pulled Dominique in close to him. At the table he'd just vacated, the two women were laughing it up with Bruno. I went through the arch and back into the lounge with its black leather booths and its black leather barstools. My grandmother raised her Manhattan to me in a toast. I nodded acknowledgment, and smiled, and walked toward where Mickey Tataglia was sitting at the bar, chatting up a redhead, who was wearing a windblown bob and a liquid green dress the color of her eyes. He had his hand on her silk-stockinged knee. She had in her hand, I swear to God, a long cigarette holder that made her look exactly like any of the Held flappers on the covers of *Life*. This was a night for firsts. I had never seen two women with purple wigs, and I had never seen a woman with a cigarette holder like this one. I had never danced with Dominique either; easy come, easy go.

As I took the stool on his left, Mickey was telling the redhead all about his war experiences. His brother Angelo was behind the bar, filling coffee cups with booze. I told him I wanted a Bosom Caresser.

"What's a Bosom Caresser?" he asked.

"I have no idea," I said. "Our waiter asked me if I wanted one, and I said yes, and he brought it to me."

"What's in it?"

"Mickey," I said, "what's in a Bosom Caresser?"

"Talk about *fresh!*" the redhead said, and rolled her eyes.

"Are you asking what I would *put* in a Bosom Caresser?" Mickey said. "If I were making such a drink?"

"Who is this person you're talking to?" the redhead said.

"A friend of mine," Mickey said. "This is Maxie," he said, and squeezed her knee.

"How do you do?" I said.

"This is Richie," he said.

"Familiar for Richard," I said.

"I'm familiar for Maxine," Maxie said.

In the other room, the band started playing "Mexicali Rose."

"If you want a Bosom Treasure, you got to tell me what's in it," Angelo said.

"Bosom *Caresser*" I said.

"Whatever," Angelo said. "I have to know the ingredients."

"Mother's milk, to begin with," Mickey said.

"You're as fresh as he is," Maxie scolded, rolling her eyes at me and playfully slapping Mickey's hand, which was working higher on her knee.

"Laced with gin and egg white," I said.

"Ick," Maxie said.

"And topped with a cherry," Mickey said.

"*Double*-ick," Maxie said.

"We don't have any mother's milk," Angelo said.

"Then I'll have a Rock 'n' Rye," I said.

"I'll have another one of these, whatever it is," Mickey said.

"Ditto," Maxie said.

"Hold the fort," Mickey said, getting off his stool. "I have to visit the gents."

I watched him as he headed toward the men's room. He stopped at my grandmother's table, planted a noisy kiss on her cheek, and then moved on.

"Was he really a war hero?" Maxie asked me.

"Oh, sure," I said. "He was in the battle of—"

"Just keep your damn hands *off* me!" Dominique shouted from the dance floor.

I was off that stool as if I'd heard an incoming artillery shell whistling toward my head. Off that stool and running toward the silvered arch beyond which were the tables with their white tablecloths and the polished parquet dance floor, and Dominique in her short black dress, trying to free her right hand from—

"Let *go* of me!" she shouted.

"No."

A smile on Mr. Noland's face. His hand clutched around her narrow waist.

Maybe he didn't see her eyes. Maybe he was too busy getting a big charge out of this slender, gorgeous woman trying to extricate herself from his powerful grip.

"Damn you!" she said. "Let go or I'll . . ."

"Yes, baby, what is it you'll do?"

She didn't tell him what she'd do. She simply did it. She twisted her body to the left, her arm swinging all the way back and then forward again with all the power of her shoulder behind it. Her bunched left fist collided with Mr. Noland's right cheek, just below his eye, and he touched his eye, and looked at his fingertips as if expecting blood, and then very softly and menacingly said, "Now you get hurt, baby."

Some people never learn.

He had called her "baby" once, and that had been a bad mistake, so what he'd just done was call her "baby" again, which was an even bigger mistake.

Dominique nodded curtly, the nod saying "Okay, fine," and then she went for his face with both hands, her nails raking bloody tracks from just under his eyes—which I think she'd been going for—all the way down to his jawline.

Mr. Noland punched her.

Hard.

I yelled the way I'd yelled going across the Marne.

I was on him in ten seconds flat, the time it took to race through that arch and charge across the dance floor, the time it took to clench my fists and hit him first with the left one and then with the right one, bam-bam, a one-two punch to the gut and the jaw that sent him staggering back from me. He rubbed his jaw in surprise. His hands came away with the blood from Dominique's fingernail-raking. He looked at the blood in surprise too. And then he looked at me in surprise, as if trying to figure out how some madman had got inside this civilized speakeasy. He didn't say a word. He merely looked surprised and sad and bloody, shaking his head as if wondering how the world had turned so rotten all at once. And then, abruptly, he stopped shaking his head and took a gun out of a holster under his dinner jacket.

Just like that.

Zip.

One minute, no gun. The next minute, a gun.

Dominique took off one of her high-heeled shoes.

As she raised her leg, Mr. Noland looked under her skirt at her underwear—black silk panties in my grandmother's "Sirocco" line, $4.98 over the counter in any of her shops. Mr. Noland then realized what Dominique was going to do with the shoe. What she was going to do was hit him on the other side of the head with it. Which was possibly why he aimed the gun right at her heart.

I did the only thing I could do.

In reaction, Mr. Noland bellowed in rage and doubled over in pain, his hands clutching for his groin, his knees coming together as if he had to pee very badly, and then he fell to the floor and lay there writhing and moaning while everywhere about him were dancers all aghast. Bruno rushed to him at once and knelt beside him, his hands fluttering. "Oh, God, Mr. Noland," he said, "I'm so sorry, Mr. Noland," and Mr. Noland tried to say something but his face was very red and his eyes were bulging and all that came out was a sort of strangled sputter at which point one of the women with the purple hair came running over and said, "Legs? Shall I call a doctor?"

Which is when I grabbed Dominique's hand and began running.

"A BOOTLEGGER, A NARCOTICS SMUGGLER, a hijacker, and a trusted friend of an even *bigger* gangster named Little Augie Orgen, *that's* who Legs *Diamond* is."

All this from Mickey Tataglia, who hurried us through tunnels under the club, pressing buttons that opened doors into other tunnels lined with booze smuggled in from Canada.

"He also owns a second-floor speakeasy called the Hotsy Totsy Club on Broadway, between Fifty-fourth and Fifty-fifth streets, that's who Legs Diamond is. You did a stupid thing, both of you. Do you know who arranged the murder of Jack the Dropper?"

"Who is Jack the Dropper?" Dominique asked.

High heels clicking, long legs flashing through dusty underground tunnels lined with cases and cases of illegal booze. Mickey walked swiftly ahead of us, leading the way, brushing aside cobwebs that hung from rafters along which rats scampered.

"Jack the Dropper," he said impatiently. "Alias Kid Dropper, whose real name is Nathan Kaplan, who all three of him was shot dead by Louis Kushner in a trap the Diamonds set up."

"The Diamonds," I said.

"Legs Diamond," Mickey said. "Alias Jack Diamond, alias John Higgins, alias John Hart, whose real name is John Thomas *Noland,* who all five of him will not like getting kicked in the balls by a fucking dope who shot himself in the foot."

"Richard did not shoot himself in the foot," Dominique said heatedly.

"I'm sure the Diamonds will take that into consideration when he kills you both. Or if not him, then one of his apes. The Diamonds has a lot of such people on his payroll. I wish you both a lot of luck," he said, and pressed another button. A wall swung open. Beyond it was an alleyway.

"You're on 88th Street," Mickey said.

We stepped outside into a dusky evengloam.

Mickey hit the button again.

The door closed behind us.

We began running.

WE GOT TO PENN STATION at 8:33 P.M., and learned that a train would be leaving for Chattanooga, Tennessee, in exactly seven minutes. It cost us an additional twelve dollars each for a sleeping compartment, but we figured it was worth it. We did not want to be sitting out in the open should any of Diamond's goons decide to check out the trains leaving the city. A sleeping compartment had windows with curtains and shades on them. A sleeping compartment had a door with a lock on it.

The train was the Crescent Limited, making stops in Philadelphia, Baltimore, Washington, D.C., Charlottesville, Spartanburg, Greenville, and Atlanta, before its scheduled arrival in Chattanooga at 10:10 tomorrow night. We figured Chattanooga was far enough away. The total one-way fare came to $41.29 for each of us. The train was scheduled to leave at 8:40.

A black porter carried our bags into the compartment, told us he'd make up the berths for us whenever we liked, and then inquired as to whether we'd care for any kind of beverage before we retired.

The "any kind of beverage" sounded like a code, but I wanted to make certain.

"What kind of beverage did you have in mind?" I asked.

"Whatever sort of beverage might suit your fancy," he said.

"And what sort of beverage might that be?"

"Well, suh," he said, "we has coffee, tea, and milk . . ."

"Uh-huh."

"And a *wide* variety of soft drinks," he said, and winked so broadly that any Prohibition agent wandering past would have arrested him on the strength of the wink alone. Dominique immediately pulled back her skirt, took a silver flask from where it was tucked into her garter, and asked the porter to fill it with any kind of colorless soft drink, please. I took my flask from my hip pocket and told him I'd have the same. He knew we both wanted gin. Or its vague equivalent.

"That'll be twenty dollars each t'fill dese flasks here," he said.

"We'll need some setups too," I said, and took out my wallet and handed him three twenty-dollar bills. He left the compartment and returned some ten minutes later, carrying a tray on which were a siphon bottle of soda, two tall glasses, a bowl of chipped ice with a spoon in it, a lemon on a small dish, a paring knife, and ten dollars in change from the sixty I'd given him. He put the tray on the table between the two facing seats, removed the two filled flasks from the side pockets of his white jacket, put those on the table as well, asked if there was anything else we might be needing, and then told us again that he would make up the berths for us whenever we were of a mind to retire. Dominique said maybe he ought to make them up now. I looked at her.

"No?" she said.

"No, fine," I said.

"Shall I makes 'em up, den?" the porter asked.

"Please," Dominique said.

The porter grinned; I suspected he wanted to get the bed-making over with so he could get a good night's sleep himself. We went out into the corridor, leaving him to his work. Dominique looked at her watch.

I looked at my watch.

It was already ten minutes to nine.

"I'm very frightened," she said.

"So am I."

"You?" She waved this away with the back of her hand. "You have been in the war."

"Still," I said, and shrugged.

She did not know about wars.

Inside the compartment, the porter worked in silence.

"Why aren't we leaving yet?" Dominique asked.

I looked at my watch again.

"There you go, suh," the porter said, stepping out into the corridor.

"Thank you," I said, and tipped him two dollars.

" 'Night, suh," he said, touching the peak of his hat, "ma'am, sleep well, the boths of you."

We went back into the compartment. He had left the folding table up because he knew we'd be drinking, but the seats on either side of the compartment were now made up as narrow beds with pillows and sheets and blankets. I closed and locked the door behind us.

"Did you lock it?" Dominique asked. She was already spooning ice into both glasses, her back to me.

"I locked it," I said.

"Tell me how much," she said, and began pouring from one of the flasks.

"That's enough," I said.

"I want a very strong one," she said, pouring heavily into the other glass.

"Shall I slice this lemon?"

"Please," she said, and sat on the bed on the forward side of the compartment.

I sat opposite her. She picked up the soda siphon, squirted some into each of the glasses. Her legs were slightly parted. Her skirt was riding high on her thighs. Rolled silk stockings. Garter on her right leg, where the flask had been. I halved the lemon, quartered it, squeezed some juice into her glass, dropped the crushed quarter-lemon into it. I raised my own glass.

"Pas de citron pour toi?" she asked.

"I don't like lemon."

"It will taste vile without lemon," she said.

"I don't want to spoil the flavor of premium gin," I said.

Dominique laughed.

"À votre santé," I said, and clinked my glass against hers.

We both drank.

It went down like molten fire.

"Jesus!" I said.

"Whoooo!" she said.

"I think I'm going blind!"

"That is not something to joke about."

The train began huffing and puffing.

"Are we leaving?" she asked.

"Enfin," I said.

"Enfin, d'accord," she said, and heaved a sigh of relief.

The train began moving. I thought of the train that had taken us from Calais to the front.

"Now we can relax," she said.

I nodded.

"Do you think he'll send someone after us?"

"Depends on how crazy he is."

"I think he is very crazy."

"So do I."

"Then he will send someone."

"Maybe."

Dominique drew back the curtains on the outside window, lifted the shade. We were out of the tunnel now, already into the night. There were stars overhead. No moon.

"Best to just *sip* this stuff," I said. "Otherwise . . ."

"Ah, oui, bien sûr," she said.

We sipped at the gin. The train was moving along swiftly now, flashing southward into the night.

"So you learned some French over there," she said.

"A little."

"Well . . . *à votre santé* . . . *enfin* . . . quite a bit of French, no?"

"Only enough to get by on."

I was thinking of the German who had mistaken us for French troops and who'd pleaded with us in broken French to spare his life. I was thinking of his skull exploding when our patrol sergeant opened fire.

"This grows on you, doesn't it?" I said.

"Actually, I think it's very good," she said. "I think it may even be *real* gin."

"Maybe," I said dubiously.

She looked over her glass at me. "Maybe next time there's a war, you won't have to go," she said.

"Because I was wounded, do you mean?"

"Yes."

"Maybe."

The train raced through the night. The New Jersey countryside flashed by in the darkness. Telephone wires swooped and dipped between poles.

"They say there are thirty telephone poles to every mile," I said.

"Vraiment?"

"Well, that's what they say."

"Turn off the lights," she said. "It will look prettier outside."

I turned off the lights.

"And open the window, please. It will be cooler."

I tried pulling up one of the windows, but it wouldn't budge. I finally got the other one up. Cool air rushed into the compartment. There was the smell of smoke from the engine up ahead, cinders and soot on the night.

"Ahhh, yes," she said, and sighed deeply.

Outside, the world rushed past.

We sat sipping the gin, watching the distant lights.

"Do you think Mr. Diamonds will have us killed?"

"Mr. *Diamond,*" I said. "Singular. Legs *Diamond.*"

"I wonder why they call him Legs."

"I don't know."

She fell silent. Staring through the window. Face in profile. Touched only by starshine.

"I love the sound of the wheels," she said, and sighed again. "Trains are so sad."

I was thinking the very same thing.

"I'm getting sleepy, are you?" she asked.

"A little."

"I think I'll get ready for bed."

"I'll step outside," I said, and started to get up.

"No, stay," she said, and then, "It's dark."

She rose, reached up to the overhead rack, and took down her suitcase. She snapped open the locks, and lifted the lid. She reached behind her, then, and unbuttoned the buttons at the back of her dress and pulled the dress up over her head.

I turned away, toward the windows.

We were coming through a stretch of farmland, lights only in the far distance now, nothing close to the tracks. The single closed window reflected Dominique in black lingerie from my grandmother's "Flirty Flapper" line, rolled black seamed silk stockings, black lace-edged bra designed to flatten her breasts, black lace-edged tap pants.

The blackness of the night reflected her.

"Pour me some more gin, please," she said.

Softly.

I spooned ice into her glass, unscrewed the flask's top, poured gin over the ice. Silver spilled from silver onto silver. Behind me, there was the rustle of silk.

"A little lemon, please," she said.

In the reflecting window, she was naked now. Pale as starlight.

She took a nightgown out of the suitcase.

I squeezed another quarter-lemon, dropped it into the glass. I squirted soda into the glass. She dropped the nightgown over her head. It slid down past her breasts and hips and thighs.

I turned to her, she turned to me. In the nightgown, she looked almost medieval. The gown was either silk or rayon, as white as snow, its yoke neck trimmed with white lace. My grandmother's "Sleeptite" line.

I handed Dominique her drink.

"Thank you," she said, and looked at my empty glass on the table. "None for you?" she asked.

"I think I've had enough."

"Just a sip," she said. "To drink a toast. I can't drink a toast all alone."

I dropped some ice into my glass, poured a little gin over it.

She raised her glass.

"To now," she said.

"There's no such thing," I said.

"Tonight, then. There is surely tonight."

"Yes. I suppose."

"Will you drink to tonight, then?"

"To tonight," I said.

"And to us."

I looked at her.

"To us, Richard."

"To us," I said.

We drank.

"Doesn't this table move out of the way?" she asked.

"I think it folds down," I said.

"Can you fold it down?"

"If you like."

"Well, I think it's in the way, don't you?"

"I guess it is."

"Well, then, please fold it down, Richard."

I moved everything from the table to the wide sill just inside the window. I got on my knees then, looked under the table, figured out how the hinge and clasp mechanism worked, and lowered the top.

"*Voilà!*" Dominique said triumphantly.

I picked up my drink from the windowsill. We both sat, Dominique on one bed, I on the other, facing each other, our knees almost touching. Outside, the countryside rolled by, an occasional light splintering the dark.

"I wish we had music," she said. "We could dance again. There's enough room for dancing now, don't you think? With the table down?"

I looked at her skeptically; the space between the beds was perhaps three feet wide by six feet long.

"Without being interrupted this time," she said, and tossed her head and began swaying from side to side.

"I shouldn't have let him cut in," I said.

"Well, how could you have known?"

"I saw his eyes."

"Behind you? When he was cutting in?"

"Earlier. I should have known. Seeing those eyes."

"Dance with me now," she said, and held out her arms.

"We don't have music," I said.

She moved in close against me.

The soft silken feel of her.

"Ja-Da," she sang.

Slowly.

Very slowly.

"Ja-Da . . ."

Not at all in the proper tempo.

"Ja-Da, Ja-Da . . .

"Jing . . . jing . . . *jing.*"

I thought at first . . .

"Ja-Da . . ."

What I thought . . .

"Ja-Da . . ."

Was that . . .

"Ja-Da, Ja-Da . . ."

Was that a fierce thrust of her crotch that accompanied each . . .

"Jing . . . jing . . . *jing.*"

I was flamingly erect in the tick of an instant.

"Oh, *mon Dieu,*" Dominique whispered.

Whispered those words in that rumbling sleeping compartment, on that train hurtling through the night, speeding us southward and away from all possible harm, lurching through the darkness, causing us to lose our balance so that we fell still locked in embrace onto the bed that was Dominique's, holding her tight in my arms, kissing her forehead and her cheeks and her nose and her lips and her neck and her shoulders and her breasts as she whispered over and over again, "Oh, *mon Dieu,* oh, *mon Dieu,* oh, *mon Dieu.*"

We brought to the act of love a steamy clumsiness composed of legs and arms and hips and noses and chins in constant collision. The train, the track, seemed maliciously intent on hurling us out of bed and out of embrace. We jostled and jiggled on that thin mattress, juggling passion, sweating in each other's arms as we struggled to maintain purchase, "Ow!" she said as my elbow poked her in the ribs, "Sorry," I mumbled, and then "Ooops!" because I was sliding out of her. She adjusted her hips, lifting them, deeply enclosing me again but almost knocking me off her in the bargain because the train in that very instant decided to run over an imperfection on the track which together with the motion of her ascending hips sent me soaring ceilingward. The only thing that kept me in her and on her was the cunning interlocking design of our separate parts.

We learned quickly enough.

Although, in retrospect, the train did all the work and we were merely willing accomplices.

Up and down the train went, rocketing through the night, in and out of tunnels the train went, racketing through the night, side to side the train rocked, rattling through the night, up and down, in and out, side to side, the train thrust against the night, tattering the darkness with a single searing eye, scattering all before it helter-skelter. Helpless in the grip of this relentless fucking machine, we screamed at last aloud and together, waking the hall porter in the corridor, who screamed himself as though he'd heard shrieks of bloody murder.

And then we lay enfolded in each other's arms and talked. We scarcely knew each other, except intimately, and had never really talked seriously. So now we talked about things that were enormously important to us. Like our favorite colors. Or our favorite times of the year. Or our favorite ice-cream flavors. Or our favorite songs and movies. Our dreams. Our ambitions.

I told her I loved her.

I told her I would do anything in the world for her.

"Would you kill someone for me?" she asked.

"Yes," I said at once.

She nodded.

"I knew you were watching me undress," she said. "I knew you were looking at my reflection in the window. I found that very exciting."

"So did I."

"And getting bounced all around while you were inside me, that was very exciting too."

"Yes."

"I wish you were inside me now," she said.

"Yes."

"Bouncing around inside me."

"Yes."

"That big thing inside me again," she said, and leaned over me and kissed me on the mouth.

VINNIE HAD BAD NEWS WHEN I called home that Saturday.

On Friday afternoon, while Dominique and I were on the train heading south, two men accosted my grandmother as she came out of her Fourteenth Street shop.

"In the car, Grandma," the skinny one said.

He was the one with the crazy eyes.

That's the way my grandmother later described him to Vinnie.

"He had crazy eyes," she said. "And a knife."

The fat one was behind the wheel of the car. My grandmother described the car as a two-door blue Jewett coach. All three of them sat up front. The fat one driving, my grandmother in the middle, and the skinny one on her right. What the skinny one did, he put the knife under her chin and told her if You-Know-Who did not come back to face the music, the next time he would be looking in at her tonsils, did she catch his drift?

My grandmother caught his drift, all right.

They let her out of the car on Avenue B and East Fourth Street, right near the Most Holy Redeemer Catholic Church. She ran in terror all the way home. Vinnie grabbed a baseball bat and went looking for Fat and Skinny in the streets. He could not find them, nor did he see a single Jewett coach anywhere in the entire 9th Precinct.

"So what do you think?" he asked me on the phone.

"I think I'll have to kill him," I said.

"Who?"

"Legs Diamond."

There was a long silence.

"Vinnie," I said, "did you hear me?"

"I heard you," he said. "I don't think that's such a good idea, Richie."

The wires between us crackled; we were a long way away from each other.

"Vinnie," I said, "I can't hide from this man forever."

"He'll grow tired of hounding you," he said.

"No, I don't think so. He has a lot of people who can do the hounding for him. It's no trouble at all for him, really."

"Richie, listen to me."

"Yes, Vinnie, I'm listening."

"What do you want from life, Richie?"

"I want to marry Dominique," I said. "And I want to have children with her."

"Ah," he said.

"And I want to live in a house with a white picket fence around it."

"Yes," he said. "And that's why you mustn't kill this man."

"No," I said, "that's why I *must* kill this man. Because otherwise . . ."

"Richie, it's not easy to kill someone."

"I've seen a lot of people killing a lot of people, Vinnie. It looked easy to me."

"In a war, yes. But unless you're in a war, it's not so easy to kill someone. Have you ever killed anyone, Richie?"

"No."

"In a war, it's easy," he said. "Everyone is shooting at everyone else, so if *your* bullet doesn't happen to kill anyone, it doesn't matter. Someone *else's* bullet will. But killing somebody in a war isn't *murder*, Richie. That's the first thing a soldier learns: killing someone in a war isn't murder. Because when *everyone* is killing someone, then *no* one is killing *anyone*."

"Well . . ."

"Don't 'well' me, just listen to me. Killing Legs Diamond will be murder. Are you ready to do murder, Richie?"

"Yes," I said.

"Why?"

"Because I love Dominique. And if I don't kill him, he'll hurt her."

"Look . . . let me ask around, okay?" Vinnie said.

"Ask around?"

"Here and there. Meanwhile, don't do anything foolish."

"Vinnie?" I said. "I know where he is. It's in all the newspapers."

I heard a sigh on the other end of the line.

"He's in Troy, New York. They're putting him on trial for kidnapping some kid up there."

"Richie . . ."

"I think I'd better go up to Troy, Vinnie."

"No, Richie," he said. "Don't."

There was another long silence on the line.

"I didn't think it would end this way, Vinnie," I said.

"It doesn't have to end this way."

"I thought . . ."

"What did you think, Richie?"

"I never thought it would get down to killing him. Running from him was one thing, but killing him . . ."

"It doesn't have to get down to that," Vinnie said.

"It does," I said. "It does."

FIVE HOURS AND THIRTY-ONE MINUTES after the jury began deliberating the case, Legs Diamond was found innocent of all charges against him.

When he and his entourage came out of the courthouse that night, Dominique and I were waiting in a car parked across the street. We were both dressed identically. Long black men's overcoats, black gloves, pearl-gray fedoras.

It was bitterly cold.

Diamond and his family got into a taxi he had hired to chauffeur him to and from the courthouse during the trial. The rest of his party got into cars behind him. In our own car, a maroon sedan, Dominique and I followed them into Albany and then to a speakeasy at 518 Broadway. We did not go into the club. We sat in the car and waited. We did not talk at all. It was even colder now. The windows became rimed with frost. I kept rubbing at the windshield with my gloved hand.

At a little after one in the morning, Diamond and his wife Alice came out of the club. Diamond was wearing a brown chinchilla coat and a brown fedora. Alice was wearing a dress, high-heeled shoes, no coat. The driver came out of the club a moment later. From where we were parked, we could not hear the conversation between Alice and Diamond, but as he walked with his driver toward where the taxi was parked, he yelled over his shoulder, "Stick around till I get back!" The driver got in behind the wheel. Diamond climbed into the backseat. Alice stood on the sidewalk a moment longer, plumes of vapor trailing from her mouth, and then went back into the club. We gave the taxi a reasonable lead and then pulled out after them.

The taxi took Diamond to a rooming house on the corner of Clinton Avenue and Tenbroeck Street. Diamond got out, said something to the driver, closed the door, and went into the building. We drove past, turned the corner, went completely around the block, and then parked halfway up the street. The cab was still parked right in front of the building. We could not have got by the driver without being seen.

Diamond came out at 4:30 A.M.

I nudged Dominique awake.

We began following the taxi again.

Ten days ago, a man and a woman named "Mr. and Mrs. Kelly" had rented three rooms in a rooming house on Dove Street—for themselves and their relatives, a sister-in-law and her ten-year-old son. I learned this from the owner of the rooming house, a woman named Laura Wood, who gave me the information after she identified some newspaper photographs I showed her. She seemed surprised that Mr. Kelly was in fact the big gangster Legs Diamond who was being tried "over in Troy." She told me he was a respectable gentleman, quiet and well behaved, and she had no real cause for complaint. I gave her fifty dollars and asked her not to mention that a reporter had been there.

The taxi took Diamond there now.

Sixty-seven Dove Street.

Diamond got out of the taxi. It was a quarter to five in the morning. The taxi drove off. The street was silent. Not a light showed in the rooming house. He unlocked the front door with a key, and went inside. The door closed behind him. The street was silent again. We waited. On the second floor of the rooming house, a light came on.

"Do you think the wife is already here?" Dominique asked.

"He told her to stay at the club."

"What will you do if she's there with him?"

"I don't know," I said.

"You will have to kill her, too, no?"

"First let me get in the building, okay?"

"No, I want to know."

"What is it you want to know?"

"What you will do if she is there with him."

"I'll see."

"Well I think you will have to kill her, no?"

"Dominique, there is killing and there is killing."

"Yes, I know that. But if you go in there, you must be prepared to do what must be done. Otherwise, his people will come after us again and again. You know that."

"Yes. I know that."

"We will have to keep running."

"I know."

"So if the woman is there with him, you will have to kill her too. That is only logical, Richard. You cannot leave her alive to identify you."

I nodded.

"If she is there, you must kill them both, it is as simple as that. If you love me."

"I do love you."

"And I love you," she said.

The light on the second floor went out.

"Bonne chance," she said, and kissed me on the mouth.

I left her sitting behind the wheel of the car, its engine running.

I tried the front door of the rooming house.

Locked.

I leaned hard on the door. The lock seemed almost ready to give. I backed away, lifted my left leg, and kicked at the door flat-footed, just above the knob. The lock snapped, the door sprang inward.

Silently, I climbed the steps to the second floor. Mrs. Wood had innocently told me that Diamond and his wife were staying in the room on the right of the stairway. "Such a quiet couple," she'd said. The steps creaked under me as I went up. A nightlight was burning on the second floor. Almost too dim to see by. A shabby carpet underfoot. I turned to the right. The door to Diamond's room was at the end of the hall. I took a gun from each pocket of my overcoat. I had loaded both pistols with softnosed bullets. Dum-dums. If I was going to do this, it had to be done right.

I tried the doorknob.

The door was unlocked.

I eased it open.

The room was dark except for the faintest glow of daybreak beyond the drawn window shade. I could hear Diamond's shallow breathing across the room. A leather traveling bag was on the floor. His chinchilla coat lay beside it. So did his hat. His trousers were folded over the back of a chair. I went to the bed. I looked down at him. He was sleeping with his mouth open. He stank of booze. My hands were trembling.

My first bullet went into the wall.

The next one went into the floor.

I finally shot Diamond in the head three times.

I came tearing down the steps. The front door was still ajar. I ran out into a cold gray dawn. A man coming out of the building next door saw me racing across the street to where Dominique was standing outside the car on the passenger side, the engine idling, the exhaust throwing up gray clouds on the gray dawn.

"Was she there?" she asked.

"No," I said.

"Did you kill him?"

"Yes."

"Good."

Across the street the man was staring at us.

We got into the car and began driving north. I was behind the wheel now. Dominique was wiping the guns. Just in case. Wiping, wiping with a white silk handkerchief, polishing those gun butts and barrels in the event that somehow, in spite of the gloves, I'd left fingerprints on them. As we approached St. Paul's Church, a mile and a half from Dove Street, I slowed the car. Dominique rolled down the window on her side, and threw out one of the guns, wrapped in the silk handkerchief. Five minutes later, she tossed out the second gun, wrapped in another handkerchief. We sped through dawn. In Saugerties, a uniformed policeman looked up in surprise as we raced through the deserted main street of the town.

We were free again.

But not because I'd killed Legs Diamond.

"WHAT DO YOU MEAN?" I asked Vinnie on the phone.

"It's okay," he said. "Somebody talked to the goons who scared your grandmother."

"What do you mean? Who? Talked to them about *what*?"

"About you and Dom."

"*Who* did?"

"Mickey Tataglia. He went to see them and convinced them you're not worth bothering with."

"But Diamond is dead. Why would they . . . ?"

"Yeah, somebody killed him, what a pity."

"So why would they be willing to forget . . . ?"

"Well, I think some money changed hands."

"How much money?"

"I don't know how much."

"You do know, Vinnie."

"I think maybe five thousand."

"Where'd the money come from?"

"I don't know."

"Whose money was it, Vinnie?"

The line went silent.

"Vinnie?"

More silence.

"Vinnie, was it Grandma's money? The money she's been saving for another shop?"

"I don't think it was her money. Let's just say *somebody* gave Mickey the money and he gave it to the goons, and you don't have to worry about anything anymore. Come on home."

"Who gave Mickey the money?"

"I have no idea. Come on home."

"*Whoever's* money it was, Vinnie . . . tell him I'll pay it all back one day."

"I'll tell him. Now come home, you and Dom."

"Vinnie?" I said. "Thank you very much."

"Come on, for what?" he said, and hung up.

When I told Dominique about the phone conversation, she said, "So you killed him for nothing."

I should have picked up on the word *you*.

But, after all, *she* hadn't killed anyone, had she?

"I killed him because I love you," I said.

"*Alors, merci beaucoup,*" she said. "But money would have done it just as well, eh?"

A week after we got back to the city, Dominique told me that what we'd enjoyed together on the way to Chattanooga had been very nice, *bien sûr*, but she could never live with a man who had done murder, eh? However noble the cause. *En tout cas*, it was time she went back to Paris to make her home again in the land she loved.

"*Tu comprends, mon chéri?*" she said.

No, I wanted to say, I don't understand.

I thought we loved each other, I wanted to say.

That night on the train . . .

I thought it would last forever, you know?

I thought Legs Diamond would be our costar forever. We would run from him through all eternity, locked in embrace as he pursued us relentlessly and in vain. We would marry and we would have children and I would become rich and famous and Dominique would stay young and beautiful forever and our love would remain steadfast and true—but only because we would forever be running from Legs. That would be the steadily unifying force in our lives. Running from Legs.

We kissed good-bye.

We promised to stay in touch.

I never heard from her again.

Walter Satterthwait is the author of eight mystery novels, most of them featuring Joshua Croft. His latest book is *Accustomed to the Dark*. His story, "The Cassoulet," is a cozy with a very dark twist, centering on an unusual circle of friends who mix cuisine and cheating at every turn.

The Cassoulet
WALTER SATTERTHWAIT

"I must speak with you," says Pascal, "regarding a matter of great importance."

"And which matter," I ask him, "might that be?"

Thoughtfully, using forefinger and thumb, he strokes his mustache. "The cassoulet," he says.

"Ah," I say, and within my chest my heart dips a few melancholy millimeters.

We are drinking Pascal's passable filtered coffee in his somewhat too elaborate dining room. The room is situated in a corner of his apartment, and the apartment itself on the top floor of a portly old building along the Quai de Gesvres. A pair of wide windows, running from ceiling to floor, afford us an uninterrupted view of the Île de la Cité and of Notre Dame with its many fine and graceful buttresses. The view no doubt is often charming; but today a gaudy sun is shining, and the river is perfectly reflecting the flawless blue of sky, as though posing for a tourist postcard; and I cannot help but find it all, as I find Pascal's dining room, a trifle overdone.

"You know, of course," says Pascal, "that I have always experienced a certain difficulty with the cassoulet."

"Yes, of course," I say. Pascal's failure with the cassoulet is renowned.

"I have never understood it," he says. As usual, Pascal is wearing black—a silk shirt, a pair of linen slacks—on the mistaken assumption that black makes him appear at once more intellectual and less corpulent.

"I believe," he says, "that I am in all other respects a tolerable cook. The cassoulet, however . . ." he shakes his head ". . . invariably the cassoulet has eluded me. At the market I have purchased the most delectable of beans, the most savory of sausages, the most succulent of pork. When I used fresh duck, I obtained the plumpest of these, and I plucked their feathers myself, with the utmost care. Always, before the final cooking, I rubbed the casserole scrupulously with garlic, like a painter preparing a canvas. Always, as the dish bubbled in the oven, I broke the gratin crust many times—"

"Seven times," I ask him, curious, "as they do in Castelnaudary?"

"On occasion. And on occasion eight times, as they do in Toulouse."

He sits back in his chair and, shrugs. "Yet no matter what I assayed, always my cassoulet lacked . . ." Frowning, he holds up his hand and delicately moves his fingers, as though attempting to pluck a thought, like a feather, carefully from the air.

"That certain something?" I offer.

"Exactly, yes," he nods. "That certain something." He smiles sadly. "You recall the party last year, on Bastille Day."

"Only with reluctance," I say. For a moment that evening, after each guest had taken a small tentative taste of the cassoulet, no one could look at anyone else. Silence fell across the table like the blade of a guillotine. Poor Pascal, who had been so embarrassingly hopeful before the presentation, suddenly became quite embarrassingly, quite volubly, apologetic.

"Yes," he nods ruefully. "A disaster."

"I have always," I say, "accounted it rather intrepid of you, this endless combat with the cassoulet."

He wags a finger at me. "Intrepid, yes, perhaps—but confess it, my friend, also rather foolish."

"Ah well," I say, and I shrug. "In this life we are all of us permitted a certain amount of foolishness, no?"

He inclines his head and smiles. "You are, as always, too kind." But then he frowns again. "You know," he says, "it was largely because of this Bastille cassoulet that Sylvie wandered out of my life."

"Come now, Pascal." I smile. "You know very well that Sylvie was wandering long before Bastille Day."

"Certainly. Sylvie was a free spirit and, I agree, a prodigious wanderer. Yet despite our many difficulties, after her wanderings it was to our life here that she invariably returned. Until the day of that fatal cassoulet. The embarrassment was too much for her. The cassoulet was the ultimate of straws."

Pascal's way with a cliche can best be described as unfortunate.

"Nonsense," I tell him. "By her very nature Sylvie was utterly incapable of fidelity."

He smiles sadly. "As you learned yourself, my friend, isn't it so?"

I return his smile, replacing its sadness with curiosity. "Surely, Pascal, you cannot hold that against me, my little incident with Sylvie?"

He lowers his eyebrows and raises his hand, showing me his pale scrubbed palm. "But of course not," he says. "It is inevitable, the attraction between one's friend and one's lover. It is, in a way, a confirmation of one's high regard for both." He shakes his head. "No, my friend, all that is history now. Water far beneath the bridge. But I speak of Sylvie. A few weeks ago, I saw her in the Café de la Paix. She was sitting with her American."

"The American is still in Paris, then?"

"Astounding, is it not? Almost ten months now, and the two of them are as inseparable as ever. You've met the man?"

"I've heard stories only. There are boots, I understand."

"The boots of the cowboy, yes. Constructed from the skin of some unfortunate bird. A turkey, I believe."

"Not a turkey, surely?"

He shrugs. "A bird of some sort. And with them, inevitably, a ridiculous pair of denim trousers. *Gray*. Sitting beside Sylvie he looked like a circus clown."

"What was Sylvie wearing?" I ask in passing.

"A lovely little sleeveless Versace, red silk, and around her neck a red Hermès scarf."

I smile. "Sylvie and her endless scarves."

"Yes. She saw me, from across the room, and waved to me to join them. I could hardly refuse, not without causing a scene. Not in the Café de la Paix. So I crossed the room, and the American stood to greet me. He's quite excessively tall, you know. He *looms*."

"It is something they all do, the Americans. Even the women. Even the short ones. They learn it from John Wayne films."

"Doubtless. In any event, we shook hands, the American and I, and naturally he squeezed mine as though it were a grapefruit."

"Naturally."

"His name is Zeke." Frowning, he cocks his head. "That cannot be a common name, can it, even among Americans?"

"I shouldn't think so." I glance at my watch. Eleven thirty now, and I have a one o'clock rendezvous at La Coupole. "So you joined them?" I say. "Sylvie and her Cowboy?"

"What choice had I? The American sat back and crossed his legs, perching his horizontal boot along his knee, so we might all admire the elegant stitchery in the dead turkey."

"I hardly think turkey, Pascal."

"Whatever. The point is the *flamboyance* of the gesture. Why not simply rip the thing from his foot and hurl it, *plonk*, to the center of the table?" Pascal shudders elaborately. "And then he hooked his thumbs over his belt, as they do, these American cowboys, and he said, *'Sylvie tells me you're in chemicals.'*

"I said, 'Not in them, exactly.' "

"Touché," I say. "In French, this was, or in English?"

Pascal smiles. "He believed himself to be speaking French. It was execrable, of course. In simple self-defense, I replied in English. 'I have an interest in a small pharmaceutical company,' I told him. 'But naturally I leave the running of it to others.'

"And here Sylvie leaned forward and she said, 'Pascal's primary interest is the kitchen.'

" *'Is that right?'* said the Cowboy. I cannot duplicate the accent. You recall Robert Duvall as Jesse James?"

"Vividly. *The Great Northfield Minnesota Raid.* A Philip Kaufman film."

"Something like Duvall. A combination of Duvall and Marlon Brando in Kazan's *Streetcar. 'Is that right?'* he said. *'I purely do admire the way you French people cook up your food.'* "

"Pascal," I say. "You exaggerate."

Indignant, he raises his chins. "Indeed I do not."

"And what did you reply?"

"I said, 'We French people are filled with awe at your Big Mac.' "

I smile.

"And then he grinned at me, one of those lunatic American grins that reach around behind the ears, and he said, *'Ain't all that big on burgers myself—'* "

"Pascal!"

"I do not invent this. *'Me,'* he said, *'I like to chow down on a real fine homecooked meal.'*

" 'Perhaps,' I said, 'one day you will permit me to prepare something for you.'

" *'That'd tickle me,'* he said, *'like all get out.'* "

"Pascal—"

"Wait, wait! Sylvie had been sitting in silence, leaning forward, her elbows on the table, her arms upraised, her fingers locked to form a kind of saddle for her chin. You recall how she nestles her chin against the backs of her fingers? How she watches, with those shrewd blue eyes darting back and forth from beneath that glossy black fringe of hair?"

"I recall, yes," I tell him.

"Suddenly she spoke. Blinking sweetly, with a perfectly innocent expression, she said, 'Zeke's favorite dish is the cassoulet.' "

"Ah," I say. "I was wondering if we should ever return to the cassoulet."

"I was, of course, stunned," says Pascal. "I had believed us to be friends still, Sylvie and I."

"Possibly your comment about the Big Mac . . . ?"

"Possibly. I was stunned nonetheless. And then the Cowboy, this Zeke creature, said, *'I reckon there ain't no food I like better than a good cassoulet.'*

"And at that point Sylvie, still the picture of innocence, sat up and blinked again and said, 'Why, Pascal would love to prepare a cassoulet, wouldn't you, Pascal?' "

"Clearly," I say, "it was your comment about the Big Mac."

"Very likely. But what could I do?"

"You had no choice, obviously, but to accept."

"None. I invited them to dinner on the following Saturday. As I said goodbye to them both, I could not help but notice in Sylvie's eye that little twinkle she gets when she is anticipating some devilment. You recall that twinkle?"

"I recall it."

"Well. This occurred on a Thursday. That afternoon, and throughout most of Friday, I pored over the literature. Brillat-Savarin. Prosper Montagné. The Larousse. On Friday evening I bought the *lingot* beans, the finest, the most expensive in Paris, and I carried them home—in a taxi, on my lap, so as not to bruise them—and I set them to soak. Early on Saturday morning I purchased the rest of the ingredients. Again, all the finest and the most expensive. And then, when the beans had soaked for exactly twelve hours, I began."

He strokes his mustache, remembering. "First I drained the beans. Then I cooked them in just enough water for them to swim comfortably, along with some pork rinds, a carrot, a clove-studded onion, and a bouquet garni containing three cloves of garlic."

"So far," I say, "the method is unimpeachable."

"Using another pan," he goes on, "in some goose fat I browned a few pork spareribs and a small boned shoulder of mutton—"

"Mutton? Pascal, this sounds ominously like the cassoulet you prepared for Jean Claude's birthday."

"The very same recipe." He nods. "I know, I know. A catastrophe."

"You are a brave man, Pascal."

"A desperate man, my friend. But to continue. When the meats were nicely browned, I transferred them gently to a large skillet, and I cooked them, covered, with some chopped onion, another bouquet garni, and two *additional* cloves of garlic—"

"Bravo."

"—as well as three tomatoes, chopped, seeded, and crushed. Then, when the beans in their separate pan were just approaching tenderness, I removed all the vegetables from them and I added the pork, mutton, onions, and a fat garlic sausage. And the preserved goose. It was while I was adding the goose that the accident occurred."

"The accident?"

"Yes." He glances at my empty cup. "Some more coffee, my friend?"

I look at my watch. Twelve o'clock. "Only a bit," I tell him.

He pours the coffee and sits back, sighing, and then with a ruminative look he stares out the tall window at the buttresses of Notre Dame.

"The accident?" I say.

He turns back to me. He smiles. "The accident, yes. It was extraordinary. Really quite extraordinary, in light of what followed. As I was cutting the leg of preserved goose, my knife slipped, and the blade went sliding along my left hand. You see?"

He holds out his left hand. Along the base of the thumb is the clear mark of a recent scar, nearly two inches long, still pink against Pascal's plump pallor.

"Impressive," I say. "Was it painful?"

"I barely noticed it at the time," he says, "so intent was I upon the cassoulet. And then suddenly I realized that I was bleeding. *Into* the beans."

"Goodness."

"I had bled rather a lot into the beans as it happens. As soon as I understood what had happened, I wrapped my thumb in a dishtowel to staunch the flow, and with a spoon I attempted to remove the blood from the beans. This was impossible, of course. Already it had mixed with the liquid in the pot. I had no choice but to mix it in more thoroughly and continue. You understand?"

"Certainly. It was too late in the day for you to begin anew. But still, Pascal . . ."

He raises his brows. "Yes?"

"It is . . . a tad macabre, don't you think?"

"Not at all. Think of blood sausage. Think of civet of hare. Think of sanguette."

"Yes, but human blood. Your own blood."

Dismissively, he shrugs. "I could not afford to be squeamish. As you say, it was late in the day. So, after having mixed everything, I simmered it for another hour, then removed the meat from the beans. I cut the meat, and I arranged all the ingredients in the casserole. A layer of beans, a sprinkling of pepper, a layer of meat, a sprinkling of pepper, a layer of beans—"

"I am familiar with the procedure."

"—and so on. Over the top I sprinkled melted goose fat and bread-crumbs—"

"Naturally."

"—and then I placed it in the oven. During the next hour and a half, I broke the gratin crust eight times, at regular intervals. By the time Sylvie and her Cowboy arrived, it was ready."

"And?" I say.

He smiles slyly. "And what?"

"You toy with me, Pascal. The cassoulet. It was a success?"

"Not a success," he says. "A *triumph*. Sylvie took a single bite and closed her eyes—you recall how she closes her eyes when she savors the taste of something, how that little smile spreads across—"

"Yes, yes," I say. "I recall." I had been recalling Sylvie rather more often than I liked. "And the Cowboy?"

"In raptures. He consumed three enormous portions. It was, and I quote, *'the best goldarned cassoulet'* he ever ate."

I sit back and shake my head. "You astound me, Pascal. A remarkable story."

"But no, there is more. Over the weekend, Sylvie and her Cowboy mentioned the cassoulet to everyone they knew. It became a *cause célèbre*. You were gone from Paris at the time."

"In Provence," I say. "I returned, as I told you, only last week."

"I began to receive telephone calls from people—occasionally from people whom I myself had never met—importuning me to prepare for them a cassoulet. You can imagine how gratifying this was to me, after my long and notorious history of failure."

"Certainly. But, Pascal. You could hardly repeat the accident which brought about your one success. The *contretemps* with the knife."

"Ah, but I could, you see."

"Pardon?"

Smiling, he unbuttons the cuff of his left sleeve. With a magician's flourish, he pulls the sleeve up along his thick arm.

Stuck everywhere along the pallid flesh are pink adhesive bandages, eight or nine of them.

For a moment I do not comprehend. And then I do.

"Pascal!" I exclaim. "But this is madness!"

Lowering the arm, he nods sadly. "I agree. I cannot continue. In the morning, I can barely climb from the bed. And yet everyone in Paris, it seems, hungers for my cassoulet."

I pick up my coffee cup, and very much to my surprise I drop it. It falls to my lap, spattering me with warm coffee, then rolls off and tumbles to the floor, shattering against the polished parquet. I look up at Pascal. "How very odd," I say.

He smiles. "The drug begins to take effect." He looks at his watch. "Precisely on time. It requires an hour. It was in your first cup of coffee."

"The drug?" Strangely, this emerges from my throat as a croak.

"A rather interesting variant of curare. A chemist at my pharmaceutical company developed it. Unlike curare, which paralyzes the body's involuntary muscles, this one leaves certain muscles untouched. One can breathe, one can blink one's eyes, one can chew, one can swallow. But one cannot otherwise move."

I open my mouth, attempt to say, "You are joking," but only a shrill sibilant hiss escapes me.

"Nor can one speak," says Pascal, and smiles. Paternally. At me, or at the drug and its effects.

I attempt standing. None of my muscles responds. Suddenly, without my willing it, my body slumps back against the chair. My head topples forward as though it might snap off at the neck, roll down my legs, and go rattling across the floor. I can feel my heart pounding against my ribs like an animal trying, frantically, to escape a trap.

"Relax, my friend," says Pascal. "You will only excite yourself."

With my head lowered, I can see of Pascal only his feet. They move as he stands up. I feel him clap me in a friendly manner upon the shoulder. Then the feet and legs disappear off to my right.

My mind, like my heart, is racing. The rest of me is frozen.

A few moments later I feel myself being lifted into the air. My head flops to the side. Pascal, for all his corpulence, is surprisingly strong. I am placed in what I recognize as a wheelchair. My head lolls back, and I have a view of Pascal's ceiling, and then of Pascal's face as he leans into my line of vision.

"Believe me," he says with an upside-down smile, "this will all go better for you if you simply accept it."

His face vanishes, and the ceiling unscrolls above me as he wheels me from the dining room.

"Perhaps you are asking yourself," I hear him say, "why I should choose you as the source of my—well, let us call it my *special seasoning*.

"First of all," he says, "you commend yourself to this purpose by the sheer emptiness of your life. No one will miss you. No one will ever even suspect that you are gone. Oh, here and there, I imagine, some poor benighted secretary, some simple-minded shopgirl, may wonder why you never telephone. But she will survive this."

We are in another room now. I feel Pascal lift me once again. The ceiling lurches, sways, and then I am lying on a bed. I feel Pascal's hand on my head as he swivels it, gently, to face him.

He stands back, pursing his lips. "And second," he says, "I confess that I have never been terribly fond of you. Your condescension, your arrogance. That metabolism of yours that permits you to eat whatever you like without gaining a gram. Insufferable. And of course there is your seduction of Sylvie. Her relationship with me was never the same afterward. You are as much responsible for her leaving me as that cassoulet of Bastille Day."

I want to cry out that it had *not* been a seduction, that Sylvie had been as willing as I, which is very possibly true. But no sound comes.

Smiling again, Pascal leans forward and pats me on the shoulder once more. "Please," he says. "Relax. We shall have a splendid time together, you and I. Like two beans in a pod. We shall have enormous amounts of time to discuss Sylvie. We can analyze her reasons for leaving us both, endlessly. And during the day, before I set off to gather the other ingredients of the cassoulet, I shall prop you up against the pillows, and you can watch the television. Game shows, soap operas. Not your usual fare, I suspect, but it will be great fun, eh?"

He stands upright. "And you need have no fear. I will never take more from you than you can afford to give. A pint here, a pint there. I am not a barbarian. And naturally, to keep up your strength, I shall provide you with the most nutritious and the richest of foods. Tonight you will be enjoying a lovely duckling in orange sauce. With American wild rice and baby peas. A vinaigrette salad of lettuce and arugula. And, I think, a nice St. Emilion. Until then I bid you adieu."

I watch him walk from the room, pull the door shut behind him.

I stare at the door. I have no choice but to stare at the door. Inside me, horror boils.

Boils and boils and goes screaming through my brain like steam from a kettle. And then, finally, like that steam, it exhausts itself. I continue to stare at the door. And all at once it occurs to me that Pascal is, as he says, a tolerable cook. And that his duckling with orange sauce is famous. His wine cellar, of course, is legendary.

John Lutz is one author who can write knowledgably about almost anything, whether it's the hapless life of timid detective Alo Nudger or the intricacies of small-town life, he brings an approach that is always different to his stories and novels. Winner of the Edgar Award for his short story "Ride the Lightning," in the following story he and David August show what happens when the federal government and small towns try to work together.

David August is the pseudonym of David Linzee, who has written four novels and this piece, his first short story. Like his collaborator John Lutz, he lives in St. Louis, Missouri.

Toad Crossing
JOHN LUTZ AND DAVID AUGUST

Standing up on the pedals as if he were a kid instead of a sixty-four-year-old man, Mr. Fitzherbert labored to the top of the hill. Reaching it, he sat down on the bicycle's seat to coast the rest of the way. He was gasping for breath. The wind felt wonderful on his sweaty brow.

On his left was a wooded hillside with the trees putting out their first green leaves; on his right was Leman Pond glittering in the slanting evening light. And dead ahead was the ominous form of Buck Earley pacing beside his employer's black limousine.

Spotting Mr. Fitzherbert, Earley stood still and put his hands on his hips. His leather-trimmed black jacket flapped open to reveal the large pistol strapped to his ribs. Mr. Fitzherbert swallowed hard. Earley was the bodyguard for a rich man who lived in one of the big summer houses down the road, so he had a right to carry a concealed weapon; Mr. Fitzherbert just wished he would conceal it a little better.

"You took your time getting here," Earley said.

"Came as fast as I could," Mr. Fitzherbert panted as he clambered off the bike with due respect for his old bones. "What did you want to see me about, Mr. Earley?"

"Well, I'll tell you. I was walking the road checking that everything was secure when I spotted something I hadn't seen before. So I called Town Hall, and they told me you were the person to talk to about it."

Earley walked onto the berm and pointed down at the mouth of a culvert set into the road-bank. "So tell me, what is that?"

"Why, that's my toad crossing." Mr. Fitzherbert couldn't keep the pride out of his voice. He'd worked long and hard to persuade the Haverville Board of Selectmen to put in the toad crossing.

"Your *what?*"

Obviously Buck Earley didn't see the beauty and utility of the concept; Mr. Fitzherbert would have to explain. But he was used to doing that. "It's a little tunnel so the toads can go under the road instead of over it. They need it especially at this time of year, the poor little fellas."

"Oh, they do?"

"Yes. You see, they sleep all winter in the mud down by the pond. In April they wake up and head for the woods, but they're still kind of sleepy and slow. Hundreds of them used to get squished by cars on this road. Made me sad to see it."

"And you actually talked the selectmen into building a tunnel for these toads?"

Mr. Fitzherbert nodded vigorously. "They have a lot of toad crossings over in England, but I think this is the first one here in Connecticut."

"No kidding. So how do the toads know there's a tunnel? You put little signs down there in toad language?"

Mr. Fitzherbert straightened up and tucked in his chin. Obviously Buck Earley was going to be a tough sell. "This is the shortest way from the pond to the woods. Toads were using it long before there was a road here. They have the right of way as I see it."

"Yeah, well, I *don't* see it that way."

"I'm not sure what you mean," said Mr. Fitzherbert slowly. He was beginning to get worried.

Earley folded his arms and leaned against the fender of the limousine. He looked down the road toward where a dusty black county truck was parked and three men were laboring noisily with pickaxes, shovels, and a vat of hot, smelly tar. The filling of potholes was as familiar a New England spring ritual as the awakening of the toads. Earley turned back to Mr. Fitzherbert. "Your toad tunnel's gotta go. Sorry." But he didn't really seem particularly sorry.

Mr. Fitzherbert stood blinking in astonishment. "But . . . why?"

"Because it's a breach of security. You know who I work for, don't you?" He smiled thinly. "Way people like to gossip around here, you probably know all about General Somona."

Mr. Fitzherbert did. Somona had been the notoriously cruel and corrupt ruler of a small Latin American nation. When he'd been overthrown, the U.S. had granted him asylum. But there were people in his country who weren't willing to let bygones be bygones, according to the news media. General Somona needed Buck Earley to keep him alive.

"I don't see how the poor toads can be any threat to your employer," said Mr. Fitzherbert.

"Not the toads, the culvert." Earley straightened up so that he loomed over Mr. Fitzherbert. "I'm going to try to explain this to you, so listen good. Say you're an assassin. How're you going to get at General Somona?"

Mr. Fitzherbert coughed. The fumes of the road crew's hot tar were beginning to bother him. "Well, I suppose I'd sneak up on his house with a rifle and—"

Earley shook his head. "You wouldn't get near the house. I've got the whole area secured. No, the only time the general's vulnerable is when he's traveling in his car."

"Then I suppose I'd set up an ambush on some road or other."

"Not so easy. I vary my routes so you can't do that." Earley held up his forefinger. "With one exception. There's only one road to the general's house. This road. So this is where you set up your ambush. What're you going to do?"

"Do?"

"How're you gonna go about setting up the ambush?"

Mr. Fitzherbert, who had never considered ambushing anyone, was finding this conversation more and more uncongenial. "Well, I suppose I'd hide up in the trees with some sort of machine gun."

"Your rounds will never penetrate my armor plate and bulletproof glass. And when I see your muzzle flashes, I open up with my Mac-10 and neutralize you." Earley slapped the gun under his jacket and smiled grimly. "No, you got only one choice, and that's a land mine."

"Land mine?"

"You have to blow me up. Now, where you going to put it?" Without waiting for an answer, Earley pointed straight down. "You're a pro. You know what success the IRA and the German terrorists have had with culvert bombs. So you're going to cram this culvert full of explosives—"

"No, I'm not," interrupted Mr. Fitzherbert.

"You're not?" Earley looked confused. "Why not?"

"Because then the toads couldn't get through."

Earley propped his fists on his hips and shook his head. "Here's the way it's gonna be: First thing tomorrow, you and I are heading down to Town Hall. I'm gonna say the toad crossing has to be blocked up for security reasons, and you're gonna say you don't object."

"But I do object."

"A man's life is in danger and all you care about are a bunch of slimy toads?"

"Toads are not slimy," retorted Mr. Fitzherbert. "Which is more than I can say for General Somona."

"Money talks. And I bet the Board of Selectmen are gonna listen."

"Maybe. But not tomorrow morning. The board doesn't meet until the first of the month." Now it was Mr. Fitzherbert's turn to smile. "It took me over a year to get the crossing put in. It'll take you at least that long to get it closed."

Still with his fists on his hips, Earley began to pace. He looked down the road. Then he grinned at Fitzherbert. "Know what? It's five o'clock now. At six I plan to be driving the general down this road. At that time, your tunnel will be blocked off."

"That's ridiculous."

Earley pointed at the county truck and the men filling in the pothole. "Here's a work crew. They can take care of it."

"But they work for the county! You can't just—"

Putting two fingers in his mouth, Earley whistled shrilly. A man who was leaning on his shovel looked up at the noise. Earley waved him over. The man put down the shovel and started walking in their direction. People tended not to ignore Buck Earley.

"They—they won't do it!" stammered Mr. Fitzherbert. "Not without an order from the board!"

"Sure they will," said Earley as he took out his wallet.

He was right. Money talked. It said emphatically that within an hour the toad crossing tunnel would be blocked.

LEAVING HIS BICYCLE TO FALL over with a clatter, Mr. Fitzherbert rushed into his cottage. He'd pedaled home as fast as he could, but he knew that Town Hall would be closed by now. But he was able to catch the First Selectwoman, Harriet Dorr, at home. He told her what had happened, pausing only to gasp for breath. "They were doing it as I left, Harriet! They were wheeling up the hot tar."

"And this was on Leman Pond Road, you said? This is all very strange. I didn't even know there was a crew working there today."

"Harriet, they were *there*. I saw them. Now, the question is, are you going to stand for—"

She wasn't listening. "Leman Pond Road. I'm going to have to check on this. Hold for a minute."

Mr. Fitzherbert stood there gripping the receiver. It was a quiet evening, and he could hear the church bells in the village tolling six. He didn't doubt that Buck Earley would be right on schedule. Even now he was behind the wheel of the limousine with his employer comfortably ensconced behind him, driving down Leman Pond Road. Perhaps he would have the pleasure of personally crushing a few toads under his tires. The thought made Mr. Fitzherbert's blood boil.

Harriet Dorr was back, rustling papers and sounding confused. "I was right. There was no crew working Leman Pond Road today."

"There wasn't? Then who were they?"

"Also I've been looking at the work orders, and there are no potholes anywhere near your toad crossing."

"Harriet, I saw them filling in a hole. Now what're you going to tell me, that they dug it themselves?"

"They must have because there was no hole there."

"Why would they do that?"

As he said the words, the obvious answer came to him: *to bury something*.

In the next instant he heard the explosion—a deep, faraway boom. It rattled the teacups in Mr. Fitzherbert's cupboards.

As soon as the police reopened Leman Pond Road, Mr. Fitzherbert went out there taking along two young friends with pickaxes. As they worked to break open the entrances to the culvert, Mr. Fitzherbert brooded. He felt a bit guilty about Buck Earley and his employer; there was no doubt that in the argument over the toad crossing Mr. Fitzherbert had provided the Hit Team—as the newspaper called them—with a perfect distraction while they placed their mine. But after all, it had been inadvertent.

Mr. Fitzherbert was pleased that it took only a few minutes' work to open the toad tunnel again. The Hit Team hadn't done a very good job of filling in the entrances.

Perhaps they were toad fanciers, too.

Sam Pizzo is a regular contributor to *Alfred Hitchcock's Mystery Magazine*, with two stories appearing there last year. A native of California, he skewers modern-day conveniences with a razor-sharp wit. In "Wild Horses," he takes on the Internet from the view of a man who uses it to escape his mundane life. Unfortunately, the net holds more than he bargained for.

Wild Horses

SAM PIZZO

In the chat rooms on the Internet, Wendell was anything he wanted to be. Sitting at his computer, he was a fighter pilot, a brain surgeon, a trash collector, a university professor, whatever tickled his fancy. Yesterday he was a lifeguard who refused, with modesty, to tell his chat room companions how many lives he had saved but admitted reluctantly there were many. The day before, he was the CEO of a Dutch multinational corporation who resigned his position and donated his stock to the company rather than lay off two thousand employees. The Internet had freed Wendell from the constraints and boredom of everyday life.

Of course, he was living a lie. Wendell knew it was wrong, but he wasn't hurting anybody, was he? He never gave advice to people online, and he never asked anything of them. He simply enjoyed being something he was not for a few minutes each day. If people online asked for advice or questioned his credentials, he would say his computer had a malfunction, or he had received an urgent call from the Vatican on his dedicated phone line. He would sign off, wait a few minutes, then sign back on and look for a different chat room.

Wendell signed on, as he did every evening, at seven P.M. His computer announced that he had mail. His wife asked, as she always did, who it was from. Wendell answered, as he always did, that it was probably somebody trying to sell him something.

Wendell guarded the password that allowed him access to the Internet. He had not written it down for fear it would fall into the hands of his wife, and she would peek into his private world. Wendell's password was committed to memory, and wild horses couldn't drag . . .

"Don't you go buying anything," said Wendell's wife. "The bills are due in a few days, and I need a new dress for the women's Jamboree and Fashion Show, and my hair is a mess, and we could afford a lot of things if you had a decent job and . . . quack, quack, quack. . . ."

Wendell tuned her out. He opened his electronic mail. It was from somebody named Tanya. Wendell had never received mail from her before, nor had he sent any. It probably *was* somebody wanting to sell him something. But Wendell always enjoyed receiving e-mail, even junk e-mail:

Dear Wendell:

You're probably wondering who I am. Well, we've never met and we've never spoken, but we see each other almost every day. I am twenty-five years old and studying to be a fashion model. I think bald is beautiful and I'm told that older men are exciting lovers. I dream of you all the time—if you know what I mean. Don't be surprised if I tap you on the shoulder some day and say, "Hi, I'm Tanya." I'm going to bed now—thinking of you.
Love, Tanya

". . . quack . . . quack . . . and quack. . . ."

Wendell committed the letter to memory, including the punctuation, then he trashed it. He had the most exciting secret of his life, and there must be no chance that somebody else would read it. Wendell reread the letter in his mind. He reread it again and again in his mind. He was amused by her choice of words, tickled by her syntax, and overwhelmed by her punctuation. Wendell was in . . .

"Quack, quack . . . Wipe that silly grin off your face. There are a lot of things you could do besides playing with that computer. The screen door has a hole in it, the cupboard doors are loose, the grass needs to be cut and . . . quack, quack, quack . . ."

Wendell walked slowly through a typical day, analyzing and cataloguing all the attractive young women he usually saw. There was the young woman who lived right down the street, the tall one with the puckered lips and long curly hair. Wendell thought of the many times he'd wanted to toot his horn and call out a cheery good morning with a casual wave, but he couldn't bring himself to do it. Maybe she was . . .

THE TALL YOUNG WOMAN WITH the puckered lips and long curly hair entered Wendell's newly purchased townhouse. She approached Wendell, a provocative smile forming and reforming on her lips. Her hair bounced with each step. She stopped inches in front of him. Her breath was minty fresh.

"Hi," she breathed, "I'm Tanya."